Joe untied the cable and twisted it around his arm. With both hands he gave it a hard tug to make sure it was secure. Then in one quick move, he mounted the railing and pushed off with all the leg strength he could muster.

The box seats loomed in front of him. As he swung to the other side of the auditorium Joe lifted his legs, preparing to hoist himself over the wall of the box. But he miscalculated. Instead of going over the wall, Joe hit it. With the cable still wrapped around his arm, he desperately grabbed for the wall. But as he took hold of it, the wall itself broke away and he fell ten feet toward the floor below.

Sweat began to roll down Joe's forehead. His hands were sweaty, too, and he felt his grip loosening. His legs were dangling in midair, and only his slippery hands were keeping him from crashing to the auditorium floor far below. . . .

The Hardy Boys
Mystery Stories

Available from MINSTREL Books

127

The HARDY BOYS®

REEL THRILLS

FRANKLIN W. DIXON

A MINSTREL® BOOK

PUBLISHED BY POCKET BOOKS

New York   London   Toronto   Sydney   Tokyo   Singapore

This book is a work of fiction. Names, characters, places, and incidents are either products of the author's imagination or are used fictitiously. Any resemblance to actual events or locales or persons, living or dead, is entirely coincidental.

A MINSTREL PAPERBACK ORIGINAL

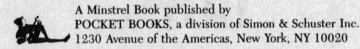

A Minstrel Book published by
POCKET BOOKS, a division of Simon & Schuster Inc.
1230 Avenue of the Americas, New York, NY 10020

Copyright © 1994 by Simon & Schuster Inc.
Produced by Mega-Books of New York Inc.

ISBN: 0-671-87211-7

First Minstrel Books printing August 1994

10 9 8 7 6 5 4 3 2 1

THE HARDY BOYS, THE HARDY BOYS MYSTERY STORIES, A MINSTREL BOOK and colophon are registered trademarks of Simon & Schuster Inc.

Front cover illustration by Vince Natale

Printed in the U.S.A.

Contents

1 Golden Princess

The roar of the blast echoed throughout the country-side, and seventeen-year-old Joe Hardy knew he was too late. The aliens had attacked the city in full force. Joe started to run, when suddenly two hands grabbed him from behind.

"Joe! Joe!" a voice called out.

Joe twisted and turned, trying to break free from the ironlike grip.

"Wake up, Joe. It's me, Frank."

Joe opened his heavy eyelids and noticed that the hands on his shoulders did not have long green tentacles. He groggily peered up and recognized his older brother's face.

"You awake, buddy?" Frank asked as he released his grip. Joe grunted and rolled onto his stomach, pulling the pillow over his head.

"I was having an amazing dream," Joe muttered

from under the pillow. He flopped back over onto his back, brushing his blond hair out of his eyes.

"Was it about an explosion?" Frank asked. The eighteen-year-old got back into his bed and gave his six-foot frame a satisfying stretch.

Joe sat up, eyes wide in amazement. "How'd you know?" he asked incredulously.

"Well, you already know I'm a brilliant detective," Frank said with mock smugness. "What you didn't know was that I'm also psychic." Frank ducked as Joe's pillow flew across the room at him "Okay, okay," Frank said, his brown eyes twinkling. "There really was an explosion. I heard it. That's what woke me up." Frank tossed the pillow back at his brother, hitting him on the side of his head. A full-scale pillow fight was about to start when the phone rang in the hallway outside the boys' room.

A shaft of light appeared under the door, and the boys heard their father, Fenton Hardy, answer the phone.

"Who'd be calling this time of night?" Joe wondered aloud. "I hope it's not about Mom and Dad's trip to France."

"I'll bet it's about a case," Frank surmised. Fenton Hardy was a private investigator who often included Frank and Joe in his work.

There was a sharp knock at the door, and then Mr. Hardy popped his head into the boys' room. "I heard the commotion in here, so I knew you were up. Why don't you guys get dressed and come with

2

me down to the marina? There's been some trouble."

After quickly pulling on T-shirts, jeans, and sneakers, Joe and Frank met their father at the car. As they drove through the dark streets to the marina nearby, Mr. Hardy filled the boys in on the few facts he knew.

"That phone call was from Mort Tannenberg, a movie producer," he began. "M.T. Productions. Ever hear of it?"

"I have," Joe said from the backseat. "They do grade B movies. You know, fast, low-budget thrillers."

"I met Mort at a party a few months ago. Seems his yacht exploded tonight and Mort thinks it was deliberate. That's why he called me."

"Does he have any idea who might have done it?" Frank asked.

"Or why?" Joe added.

"If he does, he didn't say. All he would tell me was that under no circumstances were the police to be involved."

"Why not?" Joe asked.

"I don't know," Mr. Hardy responded. "He said he'd explain it all when we got there."

Even before Mr. Hardy pulled his car to a stop in the parking area, the Hardys could see that the place was crawling with police and fire fighters. "So much for keeping the police out," Frank said. The whole western side of the bay was lit up with

3

spotlights. The boys and their father jumped out of the car and hurried toward the dock.

The smell of gasoline hung in the hot summer air. As the Hardys got closer, they saw the reason: The end of the dock had been blown away. Bits and pieces of wood and fiberglass were scattered around the bay. Frank could see why the explosion had awakened him. This had been a major blast.

"Frank, Joe, Mr. Hardy! Over here!" a familiar voice called out. Joe glanced over to the spot where police barricades were being set up and saw his friend Chet Morton waving energetically.

"I knew you guys would show up," Chet said as the Hardys joined him.

"What are you doing down here?" Joe asked his friend.

"The explosion woke me up, and I tuned in my police band radio to find out where it had happened. I figured the best way to find out what was going on was by going to the scene of the crime."

Mr. Hardy smiled. "Chet, you're going to make a good detective someday."

"Thanks, Mr. Hardy. So, do you want to know what I found out so far?" Chet asked eagerly.

"A boat blew up, right?" Joe said.

"Not just a *boat*. A $250,000 yacht named the *Golden Princess*," Chet said. "And you'll never guess who it belonged to."

"Mort Tannenberg," Frank answered.

"How did you know that?" Chet asked. Joe saw his friend's face fall in disappointment.

4

"Sorry, old buddy," Joe teased. "We're one step ahead of you. As usual."

Chet was about to protest when Mr. Hardy interrupted. "I've got to find Tannenberg. If you do any looking around, be careful."

While their father went to find the movie producer, Frank and Joe told Chet about the phone call.

"Oh, great," Chet huffed. "You've got an inside source. I had to get this information on my own."

As the three friends talked, they walked toward the end of the blasted dock and looked out onto the bay. There wasn't much left of the *Golden Princess.*

"Hey, look!" Chet said, looking down the pier. "Your dad's talking to some guy in a red bathrobe. Think that's Mort Tannenberg?"

"Let's find out," Frank said, heading for the two men.

"I heard Mr. Tannenberg tell one of the cops he thought there was just some kind of electrical short," Chet said as he hurried along beside the Hardys. "If it was an accident, then why did Mr. Tannenberg call your dad?" He suddenly came to a full stop. "Aha," he said knowingly.

Joe looked back at his friend and laughed. "Okay, Chet, I saw that lightbulb go on over your head. Now, get a move on, so we don't miss a thing."

Mort Tannenberg looked to be about fifty years old. He was of average height, with a completely

5

bald head, which made his chubby face look even rounder. Wrapped around his stout frame was a burgundy silk bathrobe.

"We were just talking about you," Mr. Hardy said as the boys approached. "Mort Tannenberg, this is my son Frank, my son Joe, and their friend Chet Morton."

The producer seemed to study the boys closely. His intense stare made them uncomfortable.

"Sorry about your yacht," Frank said finally.

Mort looked around and then back to Frank. "I want the person who did this to be sorry," he said in a harsh whisper.

"Don't worry, Mort," Mr. Hardy said. He turned to his sons. "I was just telling Mort that you'd be taking care of things for me since your mother and I are leaving for Paris in just a few hours."

Mort turned to Chet. "You're not a Hardy, are you?" he demanded.

"N-no," Chet stammered. He looked over at Mr. Hardy for help.

Joe saw his father suppress a smile. "Mort, anything you can say to me or my sons, you can say to Chet. He's helped my boys on many cases. The boys would be stranded without him." He looked at his watch. "I've got to get back. Now."

Mort grabbed Mr. Hardy's arm. "Fenton, are you sure they can handle this?"

"Trust me, Mort. There's been many a case I

couldn't have solved without them. I leave you in capable hands," Mr. Hardy reassured the producer. He patted Mort on the back, waved to the boys, and left.

"So how can we help you, Mr. Tannenberg?" Frank asked.

Mort looked the three boys over and sighed. Then he looked around the dock. "Not here," he said quietly. "At my house. I have something to show you."

Mort insisted that they meet a few blocks from the marina. From there the boys would follow him to his home. "After all," Mort cautioned, "I don't even want the police to connect you to the case."

The boys watched Mort walk quickly to his car, a silver Mercedes Benz. Frank and Joe followed Chet to his car and climbed in. They waited a few minutes so they would not appear to be following Mort.

"I can't believe we're actually going to Mort Tannenberg's house," Chet said as they made their way to the rendezvous point "The king of B-movies! I've seen them all."

At the rendezvous point, Mort flashed his lights, and then Chet began to follow him. After just a few minutes' drive, the Mercedes pulled up to a heavy iron gate. It opened automatically. Both cars pulled in, and the gate closed. After making their way down a long winding drive, the boys caught sight of Mort's house. Even in the dark they could see that it was a huge estate that overlooked the bay. Its white stucco exterior gave it the look of a Mexican villa.

Mort parked his car in front of the house and got out, taking a brown shopping bag with him. Chet parked behind the Mercedes, and the three boys joined Mort at the front door. Next to the door was an electrical push-button access code. Mort punched in a series of numbers and the door swung open.

The interior of the house was spectacular.

"Cool," Joe said under his breath as he followed Mort across a foyer with a ceramic tile floor, lots of tall plants, and tapestries on the walls.

"This place is incredible," Frank whispered.

"Awesome!" Chet agreed.

But they didn't have time to see much because Mort rushed them through an immense living room and into a wood-paneled den. Joe whistled as he saw the state-of-the-art entertainment center: a rack-mounted hi-fi system, three VCRs, and a large-screen TV.

"Make yourselves at home, boys," Mort said. He walked over to a marble coffee table and picked up a remote control. Joe sank into a plush black leather chair. Frank and Chet sat down on a long three-piece sofa also made of black leather.

"Listen up," Mort said, pacing back and forth in front of the coffee table. "What I'm about to show you must remain completely confidential."

"It will," Joe said. "You can trust us."

"I suppose I don't have much choice." Mort stopped pacing and took a deep breath. "I've been in this business for thirty years. Made over fifty movies. I've taken some lumps before, but never anything like this."

"Like what?" Frank asked.

"Like what I'm about to show you." Mort pushed some buttons on the remote control. The room lights dimmed and the entertainment center lit up with red and green lights.

"This is the final scene of my soon-to-be-released film, *The Demon Double Agent*," Mort said. "And I think it has a lot to do with what happened tonight." He aimed the remote at the entertainment center and pushed another button. The TV flickered on.

The scene opened at a marina similar to the one in Bayport. It was late at night. A woman was running away from a large yacht. As she ran, she reached up and pulled a blond wig from her head. Then she peeled a rubber mask from her face, revealing her true identity. Joe recognized her as teen star Lisa Summer.

Then the boys saw what Mort was talking about. As Lisa ran toward the camera, the yacht behind her suddenly blew up. Pieces of the yacht rained down and the picture faded to black.

"That was what we call in the business 'the big money shot,'" Mort explained as the den lights came back up. "One of my well-known surprise endings. If it was just the explosion, I'd think

9

maybe it was a coincidence. But . . ." He paused dramatically. "I found these on the dock before the police arrived."

He picked up the brown bag he had brought into the house with him and emptied its contents onto the coffee table: a blond wig and a rubber mask. Chet's mouth dropped open. Frank and Joe were equally shocked. It was the same mask Lisa had been wearing in the scene they had just seen.

2 Lights, Camera, Action

"Wow! This is too much," Chet said, staring at the wig and mask.

"Too much is right," Frank said. "Somebody purposely copied the last scene of the movie." He reached forward and picked up the mask and wig. "Not only did that person destroy your yacht, he or she also revealed that they know how your movie will end."

"Which means," Joe said, "whoever did it is somehow involved with the film."

"Exactly!" Mort sat down on the couch.

"Do you know anyone who might have a reason to do it, Mr. Tannenberg?" Joe asked.

Mort gave a hollow laugh. "More people than I can count," he said. "Look. I'm a movie producer. I make a lot of enemies. It's all part of the business."

11

"What about this surprise ending?" Frank asked. "How many people know about it?"

"Cast and crew and about a dozen of my office staff," Mort said, shaking his head. "So you've got about forty suspects." He stood up and eyed the boys. "I make my reputation on my surprise endings. If word of this hits the newspapers, M.T. Productions is sunk! This maniac would have destroyed not only my beautiful yacht, but my box office, too! I want you to get whoever's responsible and I want you to do it fast."

By the time the Hardys and Chet left Mort Tannenberg's estate, it was just before dawn. Their plan was worked out. Joe would go to work at M.T. Productions in Manhattan, while Frank joined the crew shooting Mort's current film, *Blood in the Streets*.

Back at home, the boys grabbed a couple of hours of sleep. By the time they got up, their parents had already left for Paris. After a quick breakfast with Aunt Gertrude, Frank dropped Joe off at the train station where he would board the next commuter train for the city. Frank would spend the day with Chet, trying to come up with a way to do some background checking on Mort Tannenberg and M.T. Productions.

Once in Manhattan, Joe walked the long blocks to the far West Side where M.T. Productions occupied the ninth floor of a tall office building.

He stepped out of the elevator onto a plush beige carpet that covered the floor of the reception area. A large paneled wall behind the reception desk displayed posters of Mort's films.

A young woman with curly blond hair and bright red lipstick was typing at the large reception desk. "Be with you in a sec," she said without looking up. She hit a few more keys, then turned to Joe. "Can I help you?"

"My name's Joe Hardy. I'm the new, um, gofer?" Joe said hesitantly.

The receptionist smiled. "Right. A gofer is a person who does odd jobs, either on the set or here in the office. You know, like getting lunch and delivering stuff. You just *go for* this and *go for* that," she explained. "Welcome to M.T. Productions. Long hours. Low pay. But it's show biz, right?" She laughed and stretched out her hand. "My name's Sandy."

Joe noticed that each long nail was painted a different color. "Glad to meet you," he said as he shook her hand.

"Okay, Joe Hardy, Mort told me to tell you he'd be tied up all morning and that you should see Danny DiNuccio, our office manager." Sandy pointed to a yellow door to her right. "Through that door and down the hallway. Last office on your left. Good luck."

"Thanks," Joe said as he walked to the door.

The inner hallway was quite plain, with its white walls, industrial carpeting, and more of

Mort's movie posters. Joe entered the last door on the left and found a skinny guy of about twenty sitting at a desk, looking through some papers. He had longish blond hair pulled back into a ponytail.

"Hi. You must be Danny DiNuccio," Joe said, holding out his hand. "I'm Joe Hardy. The new gofer."

Danny didn't even glance up. "I'll be with you in a minute," he said curtly.

Joe looked around the room. It was small and messy. Cans of film were everywhere.

Finally, Danny looked up. "So. What do you know about film production?"

"Not much," Joe admitted.

"Terrific," Danny said sarcastically as he stood up and walked around to the front of his desk. He was wearing baggy black pants held up by orange suspenders.

"I was the class projectionist in eleventh grade," Joe added.

"I don't believe this," Danny said, throwing up his hands. "You must have connections, right? Why else would Mort hire you?"

Joe smiled. "He and my dad are good friends."

"Figures," Danny said, disgusted. "Okay. Let me give you a tour of the place so you at least don't get lost."

Danny led Joe down the hall to a door and unlocked it with a key. The long, narrow room was lined with large 35mm film cans stacked upright on metal shelves.

14

"This is the film vault," Danny said as he and Joe stepped inside. "Every picture Mort ever made—original footage, masters, dupes, work prints—is stored here."

Danny moved down the shelves as if he were looking for something. "Anybody wants a film, they come to me," he said. "Mort and I are the only ones with the keys."

Joe noticed a partition on the far end of the room. "What's back there?"

"That's where we keep Mort's really old films," Danny explained. "The vintage black-and-whites he made with his wife, Samantha, before she died."

Danny finally found what he was looking for and pulled two large cans off a shelf labeled *The Demon Double Agent*. "Come on," he said to Joe. "It's time for your first lesson on threading a *real* movie projector."

Danny handed Joe the film cans and escorted him out of the room. The door behind them swung shut with a loud thud. Joe jumped at the sound, and Danny chuckled. "It's a special heavy-duty, self-locking door," he said. "Mort's already locked himself inside it more than once," he added with a smirk.

Joe followed Danny down the hall to a door marked Projection Booth. It was a small room with a large 35mm projector on a table in the center. Beside the projector was a control panel filled with buttons and switches. Shelves of film cans lined the booth's walls.

Through a small glass window in front of the projector Joe could see into an adjoining room. It was the screening room, and it looked just like a miniature movie theater.

"Now watch me carefully," Danny said as he opened one of the cans and pulled out a large reel of film. "If you mess it up, you could tear the film, and Mort would freak out."

Danny showed Joe how to thread the projector. Although it was much larger than the ones Joe had used in school, the process was the same.

Danny removed the reel he'd just loaded and handed it to Joe. "Okay, your turn," he said in a challenging tone. He put his hands on his hips and waited impatiently for Joe to begin.

The film path was clearly marked on the projector, and Joe had no trouble loading the film onto the take-up reel. Danny examined Joe's work. "Not bad for a beginner," he said grudgingly.

Glancing through the projection booth window Joe saw Mort and a young woman enter the screening room. Joe immediately recognized her from the last scene of *The Demon Double Agent.* It was the actress Lisa Summer. Short and slender with jet black hair, she was wearing a pink tank top and blue jeans. Joe thought she looked beautiful. She also looked upset.

Mort sat down in the first row, and Lisa took a

seat next to him. Joe could see them frowning and gesturing with their hands. Joe couldn't hear what was being said, but he could tell they were having an argument of some kind. Finally Mort raised his right hand and waved it.

"That's the signal to start the film," Danny said. "First, make sure the amplifier is on." He flipped a few switches on the control panel. "Then dim the lights with this." He turned a dial. "And then start the projector." Danny pushed a large green button on the projector and the reels began to turn.

After a couple of minutes, Danny left, cautioning Joe to be ready to load the second reel when it was time. Joe stared out the projection booth window, dividing his time between watching the movie and watching Lisa. She kept turning to Mort, clearly agitated.

Joe successfully loaded the next reel, and for the second time that day, he watched the surprise ending. When the screen faded to black, Joe turned off the projector and flipped the switch to bring up the lights.

In the screening room, Lisa looked even angrier than before. Scanning the control panel, Joe saw a switch marked Intercom. He flipped it and suddenly the voices from the other room were audible.

"How could you do this to me, Mort?" Lisa was saying. "You are ruining my career!"

"Come on, Lisa. It's not the end of the world."

17

Mort spoke quietly, but Joe could hear the impatience in his voice. "Trust me. I know what I'm doing."

"But you cut my best shots!" Lisa said. "You left out my close-ups and replaced the love scene with a motorcycle gang fight."

"Lisa, Lisa. I have to appeal to my audience." Mort reached out to put his hand on Lisa's shoulder. She jerked away and stood up.

"And you think they'd rather see Harley Davidsons than me!" she shouted.

Mort stood up, too, not bothering to hide his anger anymore. "I make the decisions, Lisa," he said with finality.

"Well, *excuse* me," Lisa sneered. Then she took a step closer and pointed her finger in Mort's face. "I'm going to get you for this, Mort Tannenberg," she warned. "I promise." Before Mort could respond, Lisa stormed out of the room.

Shaking his head, Mort watched her go. "Actors!" he said in disgust. Then he left, too.

Joe stared at the empty screening room. Was Lisa's warning just an idle threat? he wondered. Or was she really out to get Mort Tannenberg? And if she was, had she already acted on her threat?

"So, how did it go?" Danny said, breaking into Joe's thoughts as he entered the booth. "Any problems?"

"Not a one," Joe said. Turning quickly from the window, he stood in front of the control panel, blocking the intercom switch. He didn't want

18

Danny to see that he'd been eavesdropping. Trying to sound innocent, Joe asked, "What's with Miss Summer and Mr. Tannenberg? They looked like they were arguing the whole time."

"Mort fights with everybody. But it's none of your business," Danny snapped. "Put the reels back into their cans, shut everything off, and meet me in my office."

Joe's next assignment took him out of the building, delivering a package to 59th Street. When he got back to the studio, it was 12:30 and Danny had gone to lunch.

Now is my chance to do some exploring on my own, Joe thought. Mort had told them the rubber mask had been stored in the prop room. That would be a good place to start this investigation. Joe hoped that whoever had taken the mask had left behind some clues.

Wandering the halls, he found an editing room, an audio room, and a couple of empty offices. But no prop room. Baffled, he went to the reception area. Sandy was sitting at her desk eating lunch.

"Hey, Sandy, maybe you can help me," Joe said as he came up to her. She looked up and smiled.

"I'll try," she said.

"Danny mentioned something about a prop room," Joe explained. "But I can't find it."

"That's because it's in the basement," Sandy said with a laugh. "Mort rents space down there."

"I guess that's why I didn't find it," Joe said, laughing, too.

"Why were you looking for it?" Sandy asked. "Danny doesn't usually need anything kept in there."

Joe covered quickly. "I'm just trying to get my bearings," he said with a smile. "Danny had mentioned it when he gave me my minitour. Well," he added, "I'm off to lunch."

Joe was about to leave when a tall, well-built man about the same age as Mort came through the yellow door. "Be back in an hour, Sandy," the man said, striding quickly to the elevator and punching the down button. As he stood waiting, he ran a hand through his thick, wavy gray hair.

"Oh, Sid, I want you to meet somebody," Sandy called out. "This is our new gofer, Joe Hardy. Joe, meet Sid Renfield. He's been executive producer for all of Mort's films."

Joe held out his hand, and Sid shook it. "Glad to meet you, Joe," he said. He seemed preoccupied, and when the elevator doors opened, he quickly stepped inside. He punched the Close button several times, tapping his foot until the doors closed.

Joe turned back to Sandy. "If Mort's the producer, what does the *executive* producer do?" he asked.

"Oh, it's one of those catch-all titles," Sandy explained. "But it's usually someone who raises money or puts deals together. An executive producer can be a powerful studio person who hires the director and the cast. Or it can be someone

20

who puts up the money and stays in the background after that."

"So, what does Sid do?"

"Well, he used to be head of production. Now I think he's handling rereleases of the older films," Sandy said. "But I'm not really sure."

Joe thought it was a bit odd that Sandy didn't know what Sid did, but he decided not to worry about it.

During most of the afternoon Joe found himself back in the projection room logging the running time on another one of M.T. Productions soon-to-be releases: *Eternal Revenge,* a gory horror film. He spent the rest of the afternoon doing odd jobs for Danny. Finally, at 6:00 P.M. sharp, he dismissed Joe and left for the day.

Joe had one thing on his mind: the prop room. He didn't want to wait any longer in case there were some clues in there that might disappear. He suddenly realized he didn't know if the room was kept locked. *Good thing I brought my lock kit along,* he thought to himself.

Once in the basement, Joe found a door marked M.T. Productions—Authorized Personnel Only. He tried the knob and wasn't surprised to discover it was locked. *Well,* he thought, *that may narrow down the list of suspects.* As he jiggled the lock, he made a mental note to find out who had keys to the prop room. With a click, the door opened. He dropped the tool into his pocket and slipped inside, pulling the door shut behind him.

The prop room was huge, shadowy, and cavernous, with rows of tall metal shelves lining the walls. A few bare lightbulbs hanging from the ceiling dimly lit the props and costumes that jammed the shelves and overflowed into the aisles. Joe moved cautiously into the room, stepping over two large lamps and around a long, ebony coffin. *What a mess,* he thought. As he continued down the aisle, he thought he saw something move at the far end of the adjoining aisle.

Joe froze. His heart started pounding. Whoever was there knew that the door was kept locked. How would he be able to explain how he'd gotten in? Crouching down, he peeked through the shelves. He could see a shadow moving. And then it disappeared.

Before Joe could decide what to do, the shadowy figure suddenly reappeared. Only this time Joe could see it along the far wall. And it was heading straight toward him!

3 The Plot Thickens

Joe had to think fast. Swiftly and silently, he crept back to the coffin and slipped inside, lowering the heavy lid and plunging himself into darkness.

For a few moments, there was silence. Then Joe heard footsteps that got louder as they approached him. Inside the stuffy coffin, Joe felt sweat break out on his face. The footsteps continued, then stopped—right in front of his hiding place.

Whoever it was seemed to be moving things around on a shelf near him. Joe heard the sound of paper or cardboard being torn. Something clattered on one of the metal shelves and Joe's heart jumped, but he kept himself still. Finally, the footsteps began to fade. Slowly, quietly, Joe pushed the coffin lid up an inch and peered out. Danny DiNuccio was walking down the aisle and out the door.

* * *

23

"I think this is what Danny was fooling with," Joe told Frank, placing an empty picture frame on the kitchen table. "I think what I heard was the picture being ripped out."

It was later that evening, and the Hardys were in their kitchen, finishing dinner and exchanging information.

"So now we know Danny has access to the prop room," Frank said. "He could have taken the mask and may be planning something else. He's definitely a prime suspect."

"I'll keep my eye on him, Frank," Joe said. "He doesn't seem very happy at his job. Neither does Lisa Summer for that matter."

"Lisa Summer!" Chet exclaimed as he entered the kitchen carrying a large shopping bag. "What about Lisa Summer?"

"Who let you in, Chet?" Joe asked.

"Your Aunt Gertrude," Chet replied. "And she asked me to remind you guys to clean up in here when you're done." He reached across the table, grabbed a leftover french fry from Joe's plate, and popped it into his mouth.

"Thanks, Chet," Joe said, getting up and beginning to clear the table.

"So what about Lisa Summer?" Chet asked eagerly. He plopped himself down in the chair Joe had been sitting in. "Did you meet her? Is she as beautiful as she looks in the movies?"

"Yes, she's beautiful, Chet. And no, I didn't exactly meet her," Joe said. He began washing dishes. "But I did hear her threaten Mort. She told him he was ruining her career and that she'd get him for it."

"You think Lisa would blow up Mort's boat?" Chet asked. "No way!"

"We don't know what to think yet," Frank cautioned.

"Well, I brought some stuff that might help you in the thinking department," Chet said. He reached under the table and pulled out the shopping bag. The bag was filled with newspapers.

Frank picked up the paper on top. "The *Star Times?*" he said. "You read this stuff?"

Chet flushed slightly. "My *mom* reads it," he said emphatically. "And I think you may find some useful information in it."

"Like the fact that this reporter, Cindy Langly, claims that Mort would stop at nothing to get publicity," Frank said, looking at a headline.

Joe came up behind his brother and read the article over his shoulder. "But Mort said that the publicity would *ruin* the movie's chances, not help it," he said. "Besides, if he blew up his own boat, why would he hire us?"

"Maybe to throw off suspicion—so he'd look innocent," Chet suggested. "The old insurance scam."

Frank and Joe stared at each other. The case wasn't even a day old and it had already taken some strange twists.

* * *

At 7:30 the next morning, Frank's undercover assignment began. He'd be posing as a P.A.—a production assistant—on the set of *Total Annihilation*. Scenes were being shot in an abandoned warehouse in lower Westchester County, just north of New York City. Frank knew that as a P.A. he'd be assigned to do odd jobs for a lot of different people. It would be a good way to gather information.

Frank parked the van in the crowded lot and hurried to the building. The vast warehouse was abuzz with activity. In a large open space on the first floor, set decorators were placing cardboard boxes near a pickup truck parked in the center of the floor. Near the truck, Frank saw a 35mm movie camera mounted on a dolly, a small platform with wheels. He glanced up and saw, about fifty feet above, men and women adjusting lights on the rafters that crisscrossed the ceiling.

Everyone looked busy. Frank was to report to Peter Rizer, the assistant director. Glancing around, he saw two men rehearsing a fight. *They should know who Rizer is*, Frank thought, going over to the two muscular men.

They pointed to a tall, lanky young man carrying a clipboard and shouting orders to a group of workers on the rafters. Frank was surprised to see that Rizer wasn't much older than he was.

"He's kind of young to be in charge, isn't he?" Frank said. One of the stunt men snorted and the two burly men exchanged a knowing look. Then they went back to rehearsing their moves.

What was that about? Frank wondered as he made his way over to where Rizer was standing. Before he could introduce himself, Peter Rizer moved away and started giving orders to a crew member on the other side of the room. Frank followed him.

"Excuse me," Frank said. "I'm . . ."

"What? What? Can't you see I'm busy?" Rizer cut him off and turned away. "No! No! Not there," he barked at the man on the other side of the floor. "This is lunacy," Rizer muttered to himself. "We'll never be ready in time."

"Maybe I can help," Frank said. "I'm the new P.A."

"Great. Reinforcements. Where's the rest of you? Never mind." Peter abruptly turned away again and looked up to the rafters. "Hold it. Hold it," he yelled. "Why are you guys putting that cable over there? I thought I said to the left of the spotlight."

"You said to the right," a distant voice yelled back.

"Left! I said left!" Rizer screamed.

It was obvious to Frank that Peter Rizer was under a lot of pressure. He seemed ready to explode. "What do you want me to do?" Frank asked.

Peter pointed to the rafters. "Grab a pair of

27

gloves and help my crew lay cables. And make sure they get everything secure," he warned. "We're going to have people swinging from them."

My first day on a movie set and I'm going to be working fifty feet off the ground, Frank thought to himself as he headed for a scaffold.

"And who do we have here?" an older man with a trim beard said as Frank reached the top of the scaffold.

"I think Peter called me 'reinforcements,'" Frank said with a chuckle. "I'm Frank Hardy, the new P.A."

"Great," the man said, wrapping a cable around a rafter. "We can use all the hands we can get. I'm Charlie Phillips. That's Rory and Maria," he added, pointing to a young man with a long ponytail and a woman of about thirty.

Frank greeted the other two, and then he got to work. He stayed on the top of the scaffold, handing cables and a few sandbags to the others on the rafters. He also listened with great interest as they talked about Mort Tannenberg's yacht.

"Who would want to blow up Mort's boat?" Maria asked, ripping a piece of tape with her teeth.

"Well, I can think of a few people," Rory said with a smile. Frank moved closer to the edge of the scaffold, eager to hear what Rory had to say.

"But I think it was Mort," Rory went on. "He's crazy enough to have done it himself."

Maria looked over to Frank. "Don't listen to

28

Rory. Mort Tannenberg may not be Mr. Nice, but he's no mad bomber. It was probably just an accident."

Charlie hefted a sandbag on top of a cable, then joined in the conversation. "I'm not so sure of that," he said. "I heard that Mort is in deep financial trouble. The critics hated *The Demon Double Agent,* so maybe he decided to pull off some big publicity stunt to hype the film."

"Yeah. And he's probably going to collect a fortune in insurance," Rory suggested.

"You guys are crazy," Maria said, wrapping some heavy tape around a rafter to keep a cable in place.

"What do you think, Frank?" Rory asked.

"Hey, I'm new here," Frank answered. "I really don't know very much about Mort Tannenberg." *But I'm learning a lot,* he thought to himself.

"We're set," Charlie said, giving the cable one last tug. "Let's head down."

The three gathered their tools and, along with Frank, climbed down the scaffold. When they got to the floor, Charlie grabbed Frank's arm and pulled him aside.

"You're new here, so let me give you a warning," he said in a low, serious tone. "Keep on your toes. Mort Tannenberg only cares about his movies. Nothing else matters to him. If he thinks you can't cut it, that's it, you're history. You could be his best friend or his great-grandmother, and he'd still fire you. Believe me, I've seen it happen."

Frank was eager to hear more but just then Peter's voice boomed, "Full camera rehearsal in five minutes. Let's warm up the lights and get ready to rock and roll!"

After a loud clicking sound, the whole area was awash in bright lights. Charlie disappeared into the bustle of activity and Frank saw the director, Sara March, walk into the center of the group. She was an intense-looking woman of about forty with short curly brown hair. Like most of the crew she wore casual clothes: a work shirt, jeans, and sneakers. The cast followed her onto the set. Now it was Frank's turn to see Lisa Summer. *Joe was right*, he thought. *She is beautiful.*

March stood near the camera and snapped her fingers a few times. The room got very quiet. "Okay, ladies and gentlemen, you all know the scene," she said. "But let's go over it one more time." She walked to the pickup truck and began describing the action. "The three terrorists are loading stolen nuclear reactor parts into the truck over here when Lisa shows up"—March moved to a spot behind some boxes, pulling Lisa with her— "over here."

"A fight follows," the director continued, "and if we can get through that much this morning, I'll be a happy camper. Places, everyone."

The actors moved to their positions—the three black-clad "terrorists" around the truck and Lisa a short distance away behind some boxes.

After a few moments, director March yelled,

"Action," and the dolly began to move. Atop it sat the camera operator, his face pressed against the eyepiece on the camera. To his left and off to the side sat the assistant camera operator, adjusting the focus of the lens as the dolly moved toward the truck. Crouched nearby was a sound person, pointing a long boom microphone toward the truck.

As Frank watched from a short distance away, Lisa sneaked up on two of the terrorists, her pistol drawn. "Stick 'em up or you're dog food," she said in a strong, husky voice. The terrorists raised their hands. "Planning on turning downtown L.A. into toast, huh? Well, not while I'm still around. Now put your hands on the truck," she ordered.

Frank stifled a laugh. *How can she say those lines without breaking up,* he wondered. *She's a better actress than I thought.*

As Lisa shoved one of the actors toward the pickup, a third actor jumped out from behind the truck. But just as he was about to lunge toward the actress, his foot caught on a wire running along the floor and he fell to the ground.

"Cut!" yelled March. "What happened?"

"I tripped," the actor said, pointing to the thin cable sitting on the floor.

"Who left that cable exposed?" March demanded.

Peter Rizer raced over and picked up the loose cable. "Sorry," he said nervously. "One of my guys must have been a little careless."

31

The director frowned at Rizer, then turned away from him. "All right, ladies and gentlemen," she said to the actors and crew. "Shall we try it again?"

The actors returned to their starting positions. The dolly was rolled back into position. As Frank looked around the set, he could feel the tension in the air. March yelled "Action" again.

The camera rolled, and Frank kept his eyes peeled, alert to any possible disasters. As Lisa pushed the terrorists against the truck again, one of the sandbags high above the action caught Frank's eye. Unlike the others, it was balanced precariously on the edge of the rafter, directly over Lisa. As he watched, the sandbag shifted and began to fall.

"Look out!" Frank shouted, darting onto the set. He threw himself at Lisa, shoving her out of the way seconds before the heavy sandbag landed with a thud right where she'd been standing.

"Cut!" March screamed, rushing over as Frank helped Lisa to her feet.

"Thanks," Lisa said to Frank with a weak smile. Dusting herself off, she turned to the director.

"I can't take working for Mort much longer, Sara," she said angrily. "He's going to pay for this!" Then she walked off the set in a huff.

Frank knew that Lisa was angry with Mort. But why would she blame him for the sandbag? It was just an accident. Or was it?

With a sigh, Sara March turned to the crew.

"Let's take a half-hour break, folks," she announced. "Be back on the set and ready to go at 10:30 sharp." She walked off, heading in Lisa's direction.

Several crew members came over and congratulated Frank for saving the young star. Another P.A. shook Frank's hand and said, "Thanks for saving my job."

"What do you mean?" Frank asked.

The young man laughed. "I mean, without Lisa, there's no film," he said. "No film, no job! Thanks again," he added as he walked away.

No Lisa, no film. Frank found the comment interesting.

Most of the crew went outside for the break. Frank followed them, hoping to pick up some new information.

"I tell you," he heard one crew member saying. "Rizer's in over his head. He's fresh out of film school and doesn't know what he's doing."

"Yeah, and he's going to get someone killed," added another.

"Come on!" Charlie Phillips exclaimed. "Give the guy a break. It's his first film. Accidents happen. I can't count the number of lights and sandbags I've seen fall, even on major productions."

"You're just saying that because you guys left that sandbag up there," the first responded.

"It wasn't us," Charlie argued. "It was Lighting."

33

"No way!" the second insisted. "It was Stunt's fault."

The crew was definitely under pressure, and Frank was beginning to see why. The sandbag was not the first accident. Was it just Peter Rizer's incompetence? Or was it something more sinister —something to do with Mort?

As the crew continued to argue, Frank decided to do some exploring. He walked to the rear of the two-story cinder-block building. He didn't see much there, just a loading dock and some wooden crates. The door was open and Frank could see lights, stands, and reflectors. He was just about to leave when a piercing scream filled the air.

The scream had come from a second-floor window. Frank rushed through the loading dock door and bounded up the steps to the second floor. He was at one end of a long hallway.

As Frank ran down the hall, a second blood-curdling scream echoed through the empty space. A shiver went down his spine. He was sure he recognized that voice. He was sure the terrified screamer was none other than teen star Lisa Summer!

4 A Haunting Scene

Frank skidded to a halt in front of a door. The name on the door told him his hunch was right. This was Lisa Summer's dressing room. Frank shoved the door open and burst into the room. Against the far wall, a large man had his muscular arms wrapped around Lisa Summer's neck in a deadly choke hold. The young actress was desperately trying to free herself.

Frank lunged for the man. But just as he did, Lisa broke loose and swung around, catching Frank with an elbow to the chest. The surprise blow knocked Frank to his knees, stunned.

Lisa immediately kneeled down and grabbed Frank's shoulder. "Are you okay?" she asked.

"I think so," Frank gasped, still out of breath.

"I'm so sorry. I didn't see you," Lisa said apologetically. "Raymond and I were just rehearsing."

35

The big man smiled, reached out a hand and pulled Frank to his feet. With his huge chest bulging from beneath his white tank top, he looked like a weight lifter.

"Hi," he said. "I'm Raymond Brown, Lisa's personal trainer."

"Hi. I'm Frank Hardy," Frank gasped, somewhat embarrassed.

"Lisa packs quite a wallop, doesn't she?" Raymond said, obviously proud of his student.

"She sure does," Frank agreed, rubbing his chest.

"Hey, aren't you the guy who pushed Lisa out of the way of that sandbag?" Raymond asked.

Frank nodded. "I saw it falling, and I just reacted."

Raymond turned to the actress. "Maybe you should make Frank here your bodyguard, Lisa," he said jokingly.

Lisa frowned. "If this crew doesn't get its act together soon, I may need one."

A loudspeaker interrupted further conversation, announcing that the break was over and actors and crew were to report to the set.

Lisa sighed. "Well, I guess we'd better go."

"I've got to run a few errands," Raymond said. "I'll see you later."

Downstairs, the cast and crew regrouped for another try at the scene. Frank stood on the sidelines and while he was scanning the rafters for other possible falling objects, Charlie Phillips nudged him.

"Look out," Charlie said. "Here comes *real* trouble."

Glancing around, Frank saw Mort Tannenberg marching onto the set. Charlie was right about "trouble." The producer immediately got into arguments with both March and Rizer. Nevertheless, after a few takes, the scene was, as March said, ready to print.

The cast and crew repeated the scene from different angles and with camera close-ups. Then March brought in the stunt doubles to do the most difficult fighting shots.

Frank was kept busy throughout the afternoon, hauling lights and cables, acting as a safety net for the stunt artists, and doing what he was really on the set to do: watching for anything suspicious. The rest of the day went smoothly, though, and by late afternoon it was a "wrap," as March said.

But when Mort pulled him aside, Frank soon learned that his day was far from over.

"Get your brother and be at my house tonight at eight," Mort instructed. "I'm throwing a party for some friends and business associates." Nervously, he looked around the set and then back at Frank. "Who knows," Mort said in a hoarse whisper. "One of the guests may be the nut we're looking for."

* * *

A few hours later, Frank and Joe stood in Mort's kitchen, loading trays with hors d'oeuvres. Dressed in tuxedos, they were posing as waiters.

"Mr. Tannenberg sure knows how to throw a party," Joe said to Frank as he refilled his tray with Swedish meatballs. "There must be a hundred people here. I just wish we didn't have to wear these ridiculous threads. We look like penguins."

"Stop complaining," Frank said, arranging shrimp around a dish of cocktail sauce. "This is the best cover we could have. No one will notice us. Come on. The guests are hungry, and we've got some investigating to do."

Frank and Joe split up, moving from room to room, group to group, serving hors d'oeuvres and trying to hear what they could of various conversations. Frank circulated around the den where most of the conversation was about Mort's yacht.

"Poor Morty. Such bad luck about his ship," a gray-haired woman was saying.

"Yacht, dear. It was a yacht," a man in a navy blue blazer corrected her.

"Whatever. It's still a shame." The woman sighed and took a shrimp from Frank's tray. "You know, he named the boat, I mean yacht, after his wife, Samantha." The woman sighed. "The *Golden Princess.* He used to call Samantha his princess. What a tragedy she died so young."

"Mandy, that was twenty-five years ago." The

man helped himself to a shrimp. "I'm sure Mort's over it by now." The woman shook her head in disagreement, and the couple wandered off.

While Frank continued circulating around the den, Joe served guests gathered around an Olympic-sized swimming pool. He had only learned one thing so far: Mort loved Swedish meatballs. Every time Joe passed by, the producer grabbed three or four from the tray.

"Better watch your cholesterol, Mort," a man in a colorful Hawaiian shirt teased the producer.

"I'm afraid I have more important things to worry about, Jerry," Mort answered seriously.

"Yeah, I heard about what happened. Tough luck," Jerry commiserated. "But the insurance is good, huh?"

Joe was eager to hear Mort's answer, but Jerry didn't wait for one. "By the way," he continued, "I've got someone I want you to meet. She's got real star power. She can sing, she can dance . . ."

"But can she kickbox?" a familiar voice joined in the conversation. Turning, Joe saw Sid Renfield.

"Sid!" Jerry said. "How's life in the executive suite? I hear you're handling the rerelease schedule. How's it going?"

Sid gave Jerry a tight smile. "Mort's keeping me busy," he said brusquely.

Mort swallowed another meatball. "It was time the old guy had a less strenuous job," he said, giving Sid a slap on the back. Sid was about to say something when Mort interrupted. "Excuse me, gentlemen," he said. "There's someone I have to see."

As Mort left, Joe held his tray to Sid. "Hi, Mr. Renfield," he said. Sid didn't seem to remember Joe. He just took a meatball and turned away, his eyes following Mort Tannenberg.

Back in the house, Frank was serving shrimp to two women in the foyer. His ears perked up when one of them mentioned Cindy Langly, the reporter whose article was in one of the newspapers Chet had brought over.

"Did you read the piece she wrote in that rag, the *Star Times*?" the first woman said.

The second woman laughed and tossed back her bright red hair. "You mean the one where she called Mort the 'Grade-B Garbage King'?"

"Yes." The first woman plucked a shrimp from Frank's tray. "What's she got against him anyway?"

"Cindy 'Poison Pen' Langly's been out to get Mort ever since he fired her," the redhead answered.

Frank couldn't believe what he was hearing. Cindy worked for Mort? Mort fired her? He held out the tray again, hoping to hear more.

"When did she work for him?" the first woman asked, spearing another shrimp with a toothpick.

"A few years ago as a script writer," the second one said. "When he fired her, she became a gossip columnist, and she doesn't miss a chance to dig up dirt on him."

The two women had emptied Frank's tray so he didn't have a reason to listen anymore. He returned the silver platter to the kitchen, then went to find Mort. He wanted to know more about Cindy Langly. He finally spotted the producer upstairs, standing alone in the hallway leading to the master bedroom, looking very upset. By the time Frank reached him, the producer's face was pale with shock. Just then, Frank heard a woman's voice coming from inside Mort's bedroom.

"Honey. Honey, come in," the voice called from the other side of the door. "Come in, honey."

"Princess?" Mort croaked. "Is that you, princess?"

Princess? Frank was surprised. He knew from the conversations he had heard downstairs that Princess was the name of Mort's long-departed wife.

Mort reached out a shaking hand and opened the door. He took a few steps into the room, then froze. Frank stopped just behind him and peered over the producer's shoulder.

The room was dark except for a stream of light coming from the balcony outside. Frank saw a woman standing on the balcony. She was wearing a black cape and a large hat with a black veil. But this looked like no ordinary woman. Through the veil, Frank could see that her eyes were glowing a bright unearthly green.

Frank didn't believe in supernatural visitations, and he headed for the balcony door. As he did, the ghostly figure raised her arms.

"Look out!" Mort shouted behind Frank.

Frank stopped, now uncertain. Mort seemed clearly terrified. Frank stared at the figure on the balcony. The ghost-woman's hands were reaching toward him, her fingers pointing straight at his heart.

As he watched, horrified, a blood-red light began to pulsate from the clawlike fingertips.

5 Bad News

"Look out!" Mort shouted again, and rushed at Frank, wrestling him to the floor.

Mort's sudden move took Frank by surprise. He managed to push the heavy-set producer off him and scramble to his feet. He raced across the room to the balcony door. It was locked. By the time he got the latch open and stepped onto the balcony, the shadowy figure had vanished. Frank leaned over the balcony wall and scanned the grounds below. No one was in sight.

When Frank reentered the room, Mort was sitting on the edge of his bed, his head in his hands. Joe was standing beside him. "What's going on, Frank?" Joe asked his brother.

"I'm not sure. Ask Mort."

Both boys turned to Mort. The producer was visibly shaken.

43

"What happened, Mort?" Joe asked.

Mort took a deep breath. "Someone tried to do it again," he said.

"Do what?" Frank asked.

"Duplicate one of my surprise endings. This one was from *Eternal Revenge.*"

"The one where the murdered woman returns from the dead and fries her killer with two bolts of lightning she shoots out of her fingertips?" Joe asked. That was the movie he had timed the day before!

Mort nodded. "When she raised her arms at you, I just acted instinctively," he said to Frank. Then he pounded his fist on the bed. "I can't believe someone would have the nerve to pull a stunt like this! Especially when I have a house filled with people."

"I heard you call her Princess," Frank said. "Why?"

Mort's expression changed from anger to sadness. "The voice. It sounded exactly like Samantha's voice. Exactly."

Frank frowned. This wasn't just someone's attempt to destroy Mort's business. This seemed personal. And there was no telling how much more personal it was going to get. "Come on, Joe," he said, heading to the balcony again. "Maybe we'll find some clues out here."

"Looks like the copycat has struck again, Frank," Joe said as the two boys stared out over the lawn below the balcony.

The boys climbed over the balcony railing and dropped down about twelve feet to the grass below. Frank got on his hands and knees and studied the ground.

"Look at this," he said, pointing to a depression in the grass. "Looks like that ghost-woman jumped down over here." He stood back up and looked around. "Whoever it was could have made off in those trees over there."

"Or dumped the cape and went back to the party," Joe suggested. "Whoever did it could be inside eating Swedish meatballs right now."

"You're right," Frank agreed. "One thing's for sure," he added, looking to the balcony above. "The 'ghost' had to be in pretty good shape to pull this stunt off."

Frank raised his hands above his head and made a leap for the balcony. His hands just reached the top of the balcony wall. "She couldn't have been much shorter than you or me," he called down as he lifted one foot, then the other over the wall. "Unless she was some kind of pole-vaulter."

"She also might not have been a she," Joe suggested. He followed Frank up the wall and back onto the balcony.

"You're right," Frank admitted. "So someone in a black cape, wired to make his or her eyes and fingers glow, climbs onto the balcony," he said, beginning to reenact the stunt. "Then she stands in front of the glass door . . ."

"Scares Mort, then jumps down off the balcony," Joe continued. "But how did this person get Mort into the bedroom, Frank?" Joe asked.

"With Samantha's voice, but the voice sounded like it was coming from inside the room, not from the balcony," Frank said as he slid the door open and re-entered the bedroom.

"Did you find anything?" Mort asked. Joe noticed the producer was pale but seemed under control.

"Maybe," Frank responded. "But tell me about the voice we heard. Are you sure it was your wife's?"

"Positive."

Frank looked around the room. His gaze stopped on an answering machine sitting on Mort's desk. "I think I know where the voice came from," he said, walking over to the desk. "The 'ghost' used this answering machine. Probably called from a cellular phone."

"One problem," said Joe. "The phone never rang."

Frank pointed to a switch on the answering machine's control panel marked Ringer On/Off. Closer inspection revealed it was in the off position. "Did you turn off the ringer, Mort?" Frank asked.

Mort shook his head. "I never do."

"Well, somebody did." Frank pushed a red button labeled Messages. "If my theory's right," he said, "we should hear the ghost's voice."

The machine clicked on. "You have zero messages," an electronic voice announced. Frank's face clouded with disappointment.

"Are you sure the voice was coming from inside the room?" Joe asked.

"Yes," Frank said, looking baffled.

"Then maybe there's a hidden speaker somewhere," Joe suggested. The boys searched the room while Mort paced. Suddenly they heard loud voices coming down the hallway.

"Mort?" a man called. "You up here?"

"I'd better get back to the party," Mort said. He glared at the Hardys. "Find out who did this," he added sternly. "And find out fast."

"Right," Frank responded. "Joe and I will get out of here before you open the door."

So no one would see them with Mort, the boys left through the balcony door and jumped over the railing and onto the lawn.

"I don't get it, Frank," Joe said as they walked across the lawn. "Why would someone have gone through all that trouble just to haunt Mort?"

"Maybe it didn't work out exactly as planned," Frank answered. "The party is spread all over the house. Maybe the ghost expected someone or a few people to be with Mort when he went into the bedroom. Then tomorrow, someone leaks the incident to, say, Cindy Langly . . ."

". . . and she writes about it, giving away the surprise ending," Joe said, finishing the sentence.

"Exactly," Frank agreed as they approached the swimming pool and the crowd around it. "It looks like the same M.O. as the yacht, but with one extra twist: the voice of Mort's dead wife."

"You know, Frank, this could be our first real break." Joe looked around to make sure no one could hear him. "Two incidents," he said softly. "Both copying the endings of Mort's films. I think I'll find out what else M.T. Productions has in the works. It could give us a clue to what might be coming next."

"Boy, do you look tired," the always-cheerful Sandy greeted Joe the next morning. Joe had dozed on the train coming into the city and was just beginning to wake up. "What were you up to last night?" Sandy asked.

"I was serving Swedish meatballs," Joe said.

"You were at Mort's party, right?"

"How did you know that?"

Sandy grinned. "Because Mort loves Swedish meatballs," she said. "He has them at all his parties."

"Sandy, tell me something. I'm confused," Joe said, sitting down on the edge of her desk. "I heard people talking about a whole bunch of movies Mort's working on. How many does he do at one time?"

"Oh, he usually has three or four in production at once," Sandy replied. "Right now, *The Demon Double Agent* is about to be released. *Eternal Revenge* is being sweetened."

"Sweetened?"

"Uh-huh. That means it's already edited and they're working on the sound stuff. You know, adding sound effects and music. And let's see," she went on, *"Total Annihilation* is being shot, *Blood in the Streets* is being edited, and *End of the Road* is a rerelease. Here," she said, handing Joe a sheet of paper. "This is a press release describing all five."

"Thanks," Joe said. "At least now I'll know what everyone's working on."

Leaving Sandy, Joe went through the yellow door and down the hall toward Danny DiNuccio's office. He studied the press release as he walked. Each film had a short description and its running time. He was familiar with the first two on the list, *The Demon Double Agent* and *Eternal Revenge.* *Blood in the Streets* was described as an adventure-packed thriller involving a double-crossing gang of safecrackers. *Total Annihilation* was the movie Frank was working on. The press release called it the ultimate in action-suspense; it was about a deranged chemical engineer who joins up with a group of terrorists to try to nuke New York. The last film on the list, *End of the Road,* was described as a rerelease of a classic mystery of international intrigue and burning love.

When Joe entered the office he found Danny in his usual mean-spirited mood.

"You're late," he griped as soon as he saw Joe.

"Sorry," Joe said, sitting in a swivel chair. "I was just talking to Sandy."

"Well, you're working for me," Danny snapped. "And today you're going to learn how to log the dailies coming in from *Total Annihilation*."

"Dailies?" Joe asked, not familiar with the term.

"Yes, dailies," Danny said impatiently. "After the crew finishes shooting for the day, they send the film directly to the lab for processing. Those are the camera masters," Danny explained. "They stay at the lab for safekeeping. What they deliver to us are called the dailies." Danny pointed to the stack of film cans. "The dailies from each day are usually screened the next day to help the director know how the shooting is going. That's why they're called dailies. Get it?"

"Got it," Joe answered.

"Good," Danny said. "And they need to be logged in." He picked up a blue notebook and tossed it into Joe's lap. "Put in the date, the reel number, the shot number, and its length. You know—the timing. Got it?"

"Got it," Joe replied again.

"Then take the reels and . . ."

Before Danny could finish his sentence, Sid Renfield came into the office. "Morning," he said briskly. "Danny, here's a list of films I need from the vault. ASAP."

"Sure thing, Sid." Danny took the list from Sid and scanned it. "Sid? What's *Deathwalk*?" he asked.

"That's an old one, Danny," Sid explained. "Probably in Mort's private collection."

50

"Okay. I'll get right on it."

Sid glanced at Joe and did a double take. "You're a pretty busy young man, aren't you?" he said. "Office worker by day, waiter by night?"

"Just trying to get enough money to go to college," Joe answered innocently. He hoped Sid believed that was all there was to it.

"Very ambitious," Sid said with a sour smile. Then he turned and left.

Danny pulled his keys from his pocket and headed for the door. Before he opened it, he stopped and looked at Joe. "I heard that was quite a party last night," he said. "You'll have to tell me all about it sometime." Yanking the door open, he walked out, leaving Joe alone in the office.

Joe sat down and started logging the film, but his mind kept drifting back to the case. Suddenly a loud crashing sound startled him. Jumping up, he pulled the door open. As he looked out, he saw Danny sticking his head out of the film vault door. He must have heard the crash, too. The two glanced at each other, and as they did, an even louder crash made them both jump. The second crash had definitely come from Mort's office. With Joe in the lead, the two young men raced down the hall.

Just as they reached the office door, Mort's voice rang out, full of fury and horror: "She's going to kill me!"

6 More Trouble

Adrenaline pumping, Joe threw open the door and rushed inside. Danny was right behind him. Mort Tannenberg was standing behind his desk, his face tomato red, clutching a thick telephone book in his hand. "She's going to kill me!" he shouted again.

"Who's going to kill you, Mort?" Sid asked. The executive producer was standing beside the desk. Across the room, the glass doors of a wooden cabinet were partially shattered. Shards of glass littered the plush white carpet along with a three-inch-thick Yellow Pages.

Mort cocked his arm. "Stop!" Sid yelled as he lunged across the desk. Joe and Danny stood in the doorway, watching the producer's tirade. Mort hurled the second phone book at the cabinet, smashing the last of the glass.

"Calm down, Mort. Calm down!" Sid demanded.

Mort sank back into his black leather desk chair. "She's going to pay for this!" he fumed.

"Who is?" Sid asked. "What are you talking about?" Mort grabbed a newspaper from his desk and flung it at Sid.

"That's what I'm talking about," Mort said angrily. Then he put his head in his hands and mumbled, "That woman will stop at nothing to ruin me."

Joe and Danny moved to Sid's side and looked down at the newspaper in his hands. It was the *Star Times,* and above Cindy Langly's byline was a headline. "'M.T. BLOWS BOAT FOR BIG BOX OFFICE BUCKS,'" Joe read aloud. "'B-Movie Producer Desperate to Lure Crowds to His Latest Bomb.'"

"Not only does she accuse me of blowing up my own boat," Mort lamented, "but she gives away the surprise end to *The Demon Double Agent.*" He shook his head. "We can kiss our box office good-bye."

Joe was confused. "I don't get it, Mr. Tannenberg," he said as he skimmed the article. "Cindy says here that the publicity will help."

"What does she know about profits!" Mort snapped. "Surprise endings are my trademark."

Joe looked at the article again. There was a photograph of Lisa that looked very familiar to him. It wasn't a publicity shot but an actual prop from a scene in *The Demon Double Agent.* Where did Cindy get that photo? Remembering the empty picture frame in the prop room, Joe glanced at Danny. *Maybe Cindy got it from the man standing right next to me*, he thought.

"Sid, Sid. What are we going to do about her?" Mort moaned. But before Sid had a chance to answer, Mort stood up and grabbed his briefcase. "I'm going to the set. We'll deal with this later," he said as he headed for the door. "And you two," he barked, looking from Joe to Danny, "get back to work. I don't pay you to read newspapers. And someone clean up this mess!" Mort slammed the door as he left.

"That's it! I've had it," Danny said, fuming. "Nobody talks to *me* like that!"

"Take it easy, Danny," Sid said with a wry smile. "You ought to know Mort by now. When he's mad, he takes it out on everybody."

Danny yanked open the office door. "Yeah, well you might be willing to take his insults, Sid, but I'm not," he said over his shoulder. Then he headed down the hallway to his office. Joe followed him.

"I've just about had it with that egomaniac," Danny continued, striding furiously into his office and tugging on his jacket. "I'm taking the rest of the day off," he told Joe. "Find something to keep yourself busy." Like Mort, Danny slammed the door when he left.

Never a dull moment, Joe thought as he went back to logging dailies. Though Sid had been surprisingly calm. After all, if M.T. Productions really did go under, he would go with it.

At noon, Joe went to a nearby deli to pick up lunch for everyone except Sid, who'd already left for a luncheon engagement. When Joe got back, his first stop was at Sandy's desk.

"Tuna on wheat toast, hold the mayo," Joe said, handing her the sandwich. "And a diet soda."

"Thanks, Joe." Sandy started unwrapping her lunch. "I hear I missed something earlier."

"You mean with Mort?"

Sandy nodded. "I was out buying some supplies, but I'm willing to bet he lost it over Cindy's story."

"Cindy's story? You mean you read the *Star Times?*" Joe asked.

Sandy pulled a copy of the paper from her desk drawer. "Every day," she said with a grin.

"Well, you're right," Joe said. "Mort flipped. And it sounded like it wasn't the first time Langly has raised his blood pressure."

"Cindy has made a career out of beating up on Mort," Sandy said. "But this time I think she went too far. You'd better deliver those," she added, pointing to the delicatessen bag.

As Joe walked down the hallway delivering lunches, he thought about what Sandy had just told him. He wondered if Cindy's next article would be about the strange haunting at Mort's house. And if Cindy really hated Mort that much, how far was she willing to go?

Joe's last stop was the sound studio, which was filled with monitors, recorders, and other equipment. "Just put it over there." Mack Clark, the middle-aged engineer, pointed to a nearby table. "I want to get through this scene before we break."

Joe set the lunch bag on the table. "Mind if I watch?" he asked.

"Be my guest," the engineer said.

"Thanks." Joe pulled up a chair and took a hamburger out of his bag.

"We're looping a few lines," Clark explained to Joe as he put on a headset that had been wrapped around his neck. "Ready?" he spoke into a microphone.

"Ready," a voice answered over the speaker.

Behind a glass window, standing in front of microphones in a small empty room, were two actors.

Clark punched some buttons on a console. "And we're . . . rolling," he called out.

A monitor in the studio played a portion of a scene from what looked to Joe like an old movie. There was no voice track. That was what was being supplied by the actors behind the glass.

"We're replacing a few lines," Clark explained to Joe. "The actors are lip-synching to the picture so we get the timing just right."

"What's the movie?" Joe asked.

Clark adjusted some buttons on the console.

"An oldie but a goodie that we're getting ready for rerelease."

"End of the Road?" Joe said, remembering the press release.

"Yep. We found some damaged audio tracks. That's not unusual for a thirty-year-old flick," Clark explained.

"So you mean you can just take the voices off and replace them with new ones?" Joe asked.

"The sound tracks are separate from the visuals," Clark explained. "You can do just about anything with them."

Joe was fascinated with the process of looping. The portion of the film was played over and over again until the actors' words matched the lips of the actors on screen.

But as interesting as the process was, it didn't keep Joe's mind off the case. Did Cindy Langly get that photo from Danny? And what were the final scenes to the other movies on the press release? *The copycat had already used two of them to harass the producer,* Joe thought. *Which one might be next?* He thought about his brother. He couldn't wait to fill Frank in on what had happened so far.

Frank had arrived at the warehouse at seven o'clock that morning. For two hours he had helped the crew prepare for a chase scene—laying cables, adjusting lights, and helping the set designer move scenery around.

He also got a lesson from Peter Rizer on operating the smoke machine that was to be used in the first scene. "There's not much to it," Peter told him. "When the director shouts 'Action!,' just flip this switch. That turns it on."

Frank examined the smoke machine. It looked like a miniature vacuum cleaner except that attached to the back was a bottle filled with fluid.

"And when the smoke comes out the front," Peter continued, "use this piece of cardboard to fan it. Gently, like this." Peter waved the board up and down very slowly. "That will push it out onto the set."

"Looks pretty simple," Frank said.

"I'll have it in position and ready to go when you need it," Peter told him. Then he rushed off to work with some other members of his crew.

Frank checked out the smoke machine one last time, then wandered to a corner of the set to watch Lisa Summer and Raymond Brown work. Lisa had come onto the set early, and when Raymond arrived, he began guiding her through some warm-up exercises.

At 9:30 Raymond gave Lisa a fatherly hug and started to leave, waving to Frank as he passed by.

"Aren't you going to stay for the scene, Raymond?" Frank asked.

"Wish I could, Frank, but I've got things to do." Raymond explained. "I'll try to come back later." The trainer looked back to his star pupil. "I'm sure

58

Lisa can handle things on her own. Right, kid?" he said to the actress.

"Right, Raymond," Lisa called after him as he headed for the door. "I'll handle it just fine."

After Raymond left, Lisa went upstairs to her dressing room. About thirty minutes later, Sara March had assembled all the actors on the set and rehearsals began. March worked with them for the next hour. With all the lights on, the set began to get extremely hot. Everyone was uncomfortable, but Frank noticed that Lisa seemed particularly nervous. She glanced around constantly and twisted a strand of dark hair around her finger. It looked as if the tension was getting to her.

Finally March gave everyone a short break. Lisa stepped outside with the others but kept to herself. Frank was sure something was bothering the young star.

A few moments later, Peter shouted, "Places, everyone!" Frank followed Lisa back inside. As the actress took her position, a makeup artist dabbed her forehead with a piece of cotton to remove the perspiration.

"Quiet on the set," Peter shouted out.

"Let's do our first take," March announced.

Lisa moved into position.

"And . . . action!" March yelled.

Before Lisa could even make a move, all the lights went out, plunging the set into total darkness.

"Cut! Cut!" March called out in the dark. "Somebody get the lights back on. And I mean now!" she ordered, the frustration clear in her voice. "And nobody else move."

"I'm on it!" yelled a voice in the distance. A tense silence filled the darkness.

"It's just a fuse," the distant voice reported. "Peter, I told you not to plug your control panel into line 3, didn't I? You overloaded the circuit."

"Sorry, Gene," Peter apologized. "I got a hundred things going. I just forgot."

In a few moments, the lights clicked back on. Frank saw Lisa sitting on a wooden crate looking very tense.

"Okay, folks," March said, "let's see if we can get through this take without a hitch. Positions please."

Lisa stomped over to her position. Frank could tell she was still tense and angry now, too. To make things worse, Mort suddenly strode onto the set. He took one look around and exploded.

"You mean you haven't even gotten through your first shot yet, Sara?" the producer said furiously. "What have you people been doing for the last three hours?"

"Give me a break, will you, Mort?" March snapped back. "I'm working with practically a skeleton crew on the ridiculous schedule you dreamed up."

"If you can't handle it, Sara, I'll get somebody who can," Mort threatened.

"Sure, Mort," Lisa spoke up. "Why don't you dump her just like you dumped everybody else who couldn't perform miracles for you?"

"Keep out of this, Lisa," Mort said sternly. She glared at him, daggers in her eyes.

"Okay, everybody," March announced, "let's get serious about this shot!"

Within minutes, cast and crew were ready. Frank moved into position next to the smoke machine.

"Remember. Keep fanning it," Peter Rizer instructed Frank. "Gently, so it settles in the right place. Got it?"

"Got it," answered Frank.

"Let's go, let's go!" Mort demanded of no one in particular.

"Roll it," Peter called out, "and . . . smoke!"

Frank flipped the switch on, and a clear mist streamed out of the machine, quickly filling the air. Frank began to fan it with the cardboard. Only about ten seconds had gone by when suddenly everyone on the set started coughing and choking.

At first, Frank couldn't figure out what was going on. But when his eyes began to burn and his throat felt as if it were on fire, he realized that the mist streaming out of the smoke machine was some kind of poisonous gas!

7 Cracking the Wrong Case

Before Frank could move, another wave of the noxious mist floated up into his face, stinging his nostrils and burning his eyes. Coughing, he turned away from the machine, grabbed a handkerchief from his pocket, and held it over his nose and mouth.

"Turn that off! It's poison!" several crew members shouted.

"Clear the set fast!" March yelled.

As the cast and crew raced for the exits, Peter yelled out to Frank, "Shut it off. Shut the smoke machine off!" Then he followed the others out of the building.

Frank dropped to his knees and groped for the machine's on-off switch. But the smoke was too much for him, so he crawled along the floor, desperately searching for the electrical wire attached to the machine. When he found it, he gave the wire a strong tug. The plug popped out of the wall outlet and the toxic mist stopped spewing into the room.

Got it, Frank thought. Then, almost blinded by the tears in his eyes, he raced for the door.

Sabotage was all Frank could think of as he made his way outside. Someone had sabotaged the smoke machine with something that smelled like ammonia.

Frank staggered out of the warehouse. He dropped to the ground and took a deep breath of fresh air.

"Frank! Are you all right?" Charlie Phillips shouted as he rushed over to help him. Peter was with him, and together they lifted Frank to his feet.

"I'm okay," Frank said, breathing heavily.

"I can't believe you stayed in there so long," Charlie said.

"Is it still going?" Peter asked.

"No. It's off. I unplugged it," Frank said, taking another deep breath of air.

"I've never seen anything like this in my life," Charlie said, handing Frank a handkerchief. "What was coming out of that thing?"

As Frank's vision began to adjust to the bright sunlight, he wiped his watery eyes with the handkerchief. They were still burning, but he was finally able to see. "It smelled like ammonia to me," he said.

"Why would anybody want to put ammonia in the smoke machine?" Peter wondered aloud.

Frank wasn't sure. It was definitely no accident. Was it the culprit's next move? The delay would cost Mort a lot of money. But something didn't fit, Frank thought. This wasn't a final scene that was being sabotaged. Had he and Joe been wrong about the copycat M.O.?

Looking around, Frank saw that the whole crew was gathered outside in front of the warehouse. Some were still coughing and wiping their eyes. Mort and Sara March were standing over Lisa, who was sitting on the ground. The actress was choking excessively, tears streaming down her face.

"That's it, Mort!" she cried out in between coughs. "I've had just about all I'm going to take of this!"

"It's okay, Lisa," Mort said in a soothing tone. "Everything's under control now."

"No, it's not!" Lisa responded angrily. Then she became hysterical. To Frank it looked as if she were overacting just a bit.

Suddenly Raymond Brown's car pulled up. As soon as he saw Lisa, he raced over to her.

"What's wrong? What happened to Lisa?" he demanded as he wrapped his arm around the sobbing star.

"Please take me away from here, Raymond," Lisa whimpered.

As Raymond helped Lisa up, she grabbed her

64

throat and coughed again. Frank wondered why she was laying it on so thick. She hadn't even been close to the smoke machine. And was it just a coincidence that Raymond showed up when he did, just in time to "rescue" Lisa?

As they headed to Raymond's car, Lisa stopped and turned back to Mort. "Remember, I have a safety clause in my contract, Mort," she said. "You're not going to get away with this. You'll be hearing from my lawyer." She coughed again. "And I mean it this time!"

Lisa slammed the car door shut. Mort stood there, fuming. His eyes darted, first to March, then to Peter. Then he looked down at his watch.

"We'll discuss this when I get back," he said to Rizer. Stalking off, he got into his Mercedes and drove away.

"All right, everyone. That's a wrap for the day," a disgusted March announced. "Peter, check out the set and see if we can go inside to get our gear."

As the crew slowly re-entered the warehouse, Frank saw Peter Rizer rush ahead. "Wait up, Peter," he called out. "I'll go with you." Frank wanted to make sure he was the first one to the smoke machine. He wanted the bottle of fluid so he could check it for fingerprints.

Frank followed Peter inside. As the assistant director opened the door, he started to cough. The odor of ammonia was still very strong.

"Maybe we'd better wait a few more minutes,

Peter," Frank suggested. "I'll prop open the door to help air the place out. Why don't you go back outside?"

"Thanks, Frank," Peter said. "I really appreciate your help. I just can't understand what happened. I set up the smoke machine myself." Shaking his head, he headed back outside.

Frank grabbed a stool and used it to prop the door open. Then he took out his handkerchief and held it over his nose and mouth. Heading directly to the smoke machine, Frank took his work gloves out of his back pocket, put them on, and carefully unscrewed the bottle of fluid from the machine. *Maybe this will give us a few answers*, he thought to himself.

Frank slipped the bottle under his shirt. There was one more thing he needed to do: check out the equipment room where the smoke bottles were stored.

The door to the equipment room was open. Anybody on the crew could have come in here at any time and tampered with the bottles, Frank thought as he entered the small room.

Frank found two boxes of smoke bottles on a metal shelf. The top box was open and there were three bottles left in it. They looked exactly like the bottle that had been tampered with. Frank unscrewed each one. No odor. So someone must have emptied the liquid out of the bottle and then replaced it with ammonia, he figured.

Suddenly Frank heard footsteps behind him.

Whirling around, he found himself face-to-face with a short woman whose long blond hair was pulled back. Her fashionable suit was a bright red in sharp contrast with the drab surroundings. A large leather bag was slung over one shoulder, and it had a cord dangling from it. Attached to the cord was a small microphone, which the woman was gripping tightly.

"I heard there was quite a fiasco on the set this morning," the woman said, pushing the mike in Frank's face. "Care to fill me in on the details?"

Before Frank could answer, Sara March entered the room.

"Cindy Langly. What are you doing here?" she said to the reporter in a less than friendly voice.

"Good to see you, too, Sara," Cindy responded sarcastically.

So this is the infamous Cindy Langly, Frank thought. He wished the director hadn't interrupted them. He had a feeling he could learn a lot from this pushy reporter.

"You know you're not allowed on the set. Mort would go into cardiac arrest if he found you here."

"Come on, Sara, give me a break," Cindy urged. "This is a great scoop."

March firmly shook her head. "Get out of here, or I'll call the security guards."

"Say please."

"Now!" March demanded.

"Okay. Okay. I'm going," Cindy shrugged and smiled a huge phony smile.

67

The reporter pretended to follow March out, then hurried back to Frank.

"I'd really like to talk to you," she said in a whisper. "How about after work, say 6:30? Meet me at the West Side Garage on 18th Street and Ninth Avenue. I'll make it worth your while."

Sara March reappeared in the doorway, glowering. Cindy scurried past her. "Ciao!" she warbled gaily.

"Ciao," Frank called after her. Sure he'd meet her, to ask her how she happened to turn up so soon after this latest incident. Or *had* she just turned up? Could she have been hiding on the set the whole time? Could Cindy Langly have sabotaged the smoke machine? From all he'd been learning, she really had a grudge against Mort.

Frank didn't have any answers. All he had were a lot more questions. He wondered if his brother was doing any better.

In the New York office, Joe was busy at work—also looking for answers. In Danny's office he'd found a copy of *Blood in the Streets*, one of the films on M.T. Production's soon-to-be-released list. It was 2:00 P.M. and with Danny and Sid out of the office, Joe decided it was a good time to screen the film. He took the reels into the projection booth and loaded the first one on to the projector.

Blood in the Streets had a typical Mort Tannenberg plot, Joe thought as he watched it. Lisa again had the starring role, this time playing a ruthless

68

safecracker ninja expert named Raven Blue. The film was long on cheap stunts and special effects, short on story.

Even though he was enjoying it, Joe waited impatiently for the final scene. It began with Raven Blue making her way through a high-tech security system filled with video cameras and laser beam detectors.

As Blue crawled across the floor, the phone in the projection booth began to ring. Joe picked it up.

"Joe. Are you there?" Sandy's voice sounded over the intercom.

"Hi, Sandy. What's up?"

"It's Mort on line three for you, and he sounds positively bonkers," Sandy remarked. "Says somebody broke into the safe at his house."

"Safe?" Joe repeated. He looked up at the screen. He couldn't believe his eyes. Raven Blue had made it through Security and was opening a wall safe. The steel door swung open and Blue reached in. She had just murdered five people to get her hands on the priceless diamond locked inside it.

Suddenly, the expression on Raven Blue's face changed from a smug smile to a horrified grimace. Instead of the diamond, she was holding a live electrical wire. Sparks began to fly and she started to shake uncontrollably.

Then the skin began to melt from Raven Blue's body.

8 Tough Threat

Raven Blue dropped to the floor, nothing left of her but a pile of smoldering bones. Joe realized Mort was still on hold. He quickly punched the flashing button on the phone.

"Hello, Mort? Joe Hardy here. I just saw . . ."

"Listen, Joe, and listen carefully," Mort interrupted, his voice tight with anger. "Someone got through the extremely high-tech security system at my house and broke into my safe. But that's not the worst of it."

"I know," Joe said, switching off the projector. "I just watched *Blood in the Streets*. It's another copycat crime."

"So don't just sit there, do something about it!" Mort bellowed. "The security system in the movie was modeled on the one that I have at home. I want some answers by the time I get back from Jamaica."

"Jamaica?"

"That's right, Jamaica. Sandy has my number."
Mort hung up.

Joe got the number from Sandy and then quickly
dialed the warehouse, hoping his brother was still
there. It rang a long time, but finally someone
answered and found Frank.

"You're lucky, Joe," he said. "You almost missed
me. I was on my way out."

"Frank!" Joe said excitedly. "You won't believe
what just happened."

"Ha! You won't believe what happened *here*,"
Frank said.

"This is really serious, Frank. I mean *really*
serious," Joe said with urgency in his voice. Just
then he heard clicking on the phone line. Was
it just a bad connection? Or was someone listening in? "I'd better not talk now," he said to
Frank. "Pick me up at the office as soon as you
can."

When Frank arrived a half hour later, Joe was
outside the building pacing up and down on the
sidewalk. "Let's go," he said as he hopped into the
van.

"Where?" Frank asked.

"To Mort's house," Joe instructed. "There's
been another copycat crime."

"*Another* one?" Frank was surprised.

"I'm pretty sure of it," Joe said. "Mort called,
furious. Someone broke into the safe at his house."

71

"So why was it a copycat crime?" Frank asked as he headed for the highway.

"Mort called while I was watching *Blood in the Streets*," Joe said. "Guess what the last scene was?"

"A break-in?"

"You got it."

Frank was silent for a moment as he tried to put the new pieces together. Two crimes in one day? Something didn't make sense.

"So what happened on the set?" Joe asked as they drove over a bridge.

"Oh, not much," Frank said with sarcasm in his voice. "Let's see. There was a power failure that left us all standing in the dark, and then the smoke machine spewed out ammonia. And that cleared the set for the day."

"Wow! Anybody hurt?" Joe asked.

"Nope. But it was clearly not an accident. Someone had tampered with the machine," Frank said.

"Any leads on who did it?"

"Well, Lisa seemed edgy all morning. Acting very strange and overacting like crazy after the ammonia incident. I'm sure of that." Frank slowed the van and paid the bridge toll. "And Raymond Brown, her trainer, left the set before the accident and conveniently returned right after it," he added, pulling the van onto the expressway.

"So what are you thinking?" Joe asked. "Lisa

sabotaged the smoke machine while Raymond broke into Mort's safe?"

"It's a possibility." With one hand, Frank reached under his seat and pulled out the smoke bottle he'd taken off the smoke machine. It was wrapped in an old T-shirt. "Maybe this will give us some answers once we check it for fingerprints," he said, handing it to his brother.

Joe carefully unwrapped it. "Phew!" He grimaced. The smell of ammonia was still strong.

"Is Mort at the house?" Frank asked.

"Nope. He's in sunny Jamaica," Joe answered.

"Jamaica? Why would he suddenly leave with all this happening?"

Joe shrugged his shoulders. "Beats me. Unless he didn't want to be around to answer any questions."

Frank had just about ruled out Mort as a possible suspect, but now he wasn't so sure.

A short while later, Frank announced himself at Mort's front gate, pulled the van down the winding driveway, and parked in front of the producer's house, behind two security cars.

The front door was open and the boys had just stepped into the house when they were stopped by a beefy security guard.

"Hold it," the guard said. "Where do you guys think you're going?"

"I'm Joe Hardy," Joe said. "This is my brother Frank. Mr. Tannenberg . . ."

"Oh, right, the Hardy boys," the guard interrupted. "Mort told me to expect you. I'm George Brandish, the chief of security for Sentry Security." George and the boys shook hands.

"Can you fill us in on the details?" Frank asked.

George led the boys into the den and pointed to the far wall. A large abstract painting, hinged like a door, was swung open and revealed a wall safe. The safe door was open, too.

"See for yourself, boys," George said. "Someone got through the front door, the video cameras, and the laser beams and into Mort's safe." He shook his head. "I can't believe it. This house is equipped with our most advanced security system, yet the perpetrator didn't set off a single alarm."

"Maybe it was an inside job," Frank suggested.

"You're not saying one of my people did this, are you?" George asked defensively.

"What do *you* say?" Frank asked.

"I say I know my guys," George told Frank. "They wouldn't do anything like this. Besides, Mr. Tannenberg said nothing was taken."

That didn't surprise Joe. Raven Blue never did get a chance to take anything in the final scene. She had gotten fried first.

"The strange thing is," George added, "whoever did it left two things behind." He held up a note and a frayed electrical cord. "I can't make sense out of these."

74

The security guard handed the note to Frank and the frayed cord to Joe.

The note was typed on M.T. Production stationery. Frank read it out loud: " 'Coming Soon: The Final Cut!' "

"Any idea what it means?" George asked the boys.

"Trouble," Joe said, twisting the electrical cord in his fingertips.

Twenty minutes later, as the boys drove away from Mort's house, Joe turned to Frank. "I think the note means what it says—that the next move is going to be the last one," he said.

"And that move could spell disaster for Mort if we don't stop it," Frank added in an ominous tone.

After a few minutes, Joe noticed that Frank wasn't heading for home. "Where are we going?" he asked.

"Back into the city."

"The city? Why?"

"Oh, I forgot to tell you," Frank said, passing a slow-moving truck. "Guess who showed up on the set just after the smoke incident?"

"Who?" Joe asked eagerly.

"Cindy Langly."

"No kidding?"

Frank nodded. "She wants to talk to me, so I'm meeting her at 6:30 in some garage downtown.

"That should be interesting," Joe said. "Why

don't you drop me off at Mort's office? I want to check out a few typewriters." He held up the note that George had turned over to them.

"Good idea," Frank said.

Traffic was light going into the city and it was 6:20 P.M. when Frank pulled the van to a stop in front of Mort's studio.

"Meet me at the garage in half an hour," Frank said to his brother. Joe waved and went inside, taking the elevator to the ninth floor, where he found Sandy getting ready to leave.

"Joe?" she said, surprised to see him. "What brings you back here?"

"Mort wanted me to get some papers from his desk," Joe told her.

"You're lucky I stayed late tonight. You'll need this." Sandy pulled a key chain from her pocketbook and held up one of the keys on it. But instead of giving Joe the key, she escorted him to Mort's office and unlocked the door for him.

"I gotta run," Sandy said, dropping her key chain back into her pocketbook. "Just slam the door closed when you leave. 'Bye."

"Thanks, Sandy. See you tomorrow."

As soon as Joe heard the yellow hallway door close, he headed for Mort's electric typewriter sitting on a small table next to the desk. He turned the typewriter on, put a piece of paper in it, and started to type the sentence: Coming Soon: The Final Cut!

Before Joe could finish, he heard voices coming

down the hall. He had no time to do anything but turn the typewriter off. Then he quickly crouched down under Mort's desk.

"What's Mort's door doing open?" Joe heard a familiar voice say from right outside the door. It was Sid Renfield. As the executive producer entered the room, Joe held his breath.

"Listen, Sid. Mort's really on my back," said another voice that Joe didn't recognize. "He cut my budget, he cut shooting days, and he still wants all the stunts and effects."

"You're not telling me anything I don't know."

From his view under the desk Joe could see someone's feet coming toward the desk. He smacked himself lightly on the forehead. *Dummy!* he thought. The note he had just typed was still in the typewriter!

"That's why I'm talking to you," the second voice continued. "I thought since you used to be in charge of production, you could help me."

Sid laughed, but he didn't sound very amused. "Sorry, Peter," he said. "It's your headache. I'm out of day-to-day operations now, remember?"

Peter, Joe thought. Frank had talked about a Peter Rizer. He was the assistant director on *Total Annihilation.*

"But, Sid," Peter went on, "you and Mort go back a long way. You know how to handle him better than I do."

"If I really knew how to handle Mort, things would be different." Sid laughed easily again.

77

"Come on. Let's get out of here." Finally, he moved away from the desk.

Joe kept still until the lights went off and he heard the door close. Then he let out a long breath and slowly got up. *That was a close one,* he thought, carefully taking the paper from the typewriter. He hoped they hadn't noticed it.

Leaving Mort's office, Joe made sure Sid and Peter were gone. He decided to go from office to office, hoping to gather other typewriter samples to compare with the note left on Mort's safe. Most of the studios and offices were locked. Eager to meet Frank, Joe decided that rather than spend the time picking each lock, he'd get the rest of the samples another time.

Frank pulled the van into the dimly lit, rundown West Side Garage.

Strange place for an interview, he thought, parking in the rear and checking his watch. It was 6:30 exactly.

By 6:45 P.M., Cindy had still not shown up. As Frank got out of the van to stretch his legs, a taxi entered the garage and pulled up to him. Cindy Langly was in the backseat.

"Hi," Frank said as Cindy rolled down the window.

"Glad you could make it." Cindy stepped out of the cab and looked around as if to make sure they were alone. "Look, Frank. I won't beat around the bush," she said. "I've got Mort just about where I want him, but I need one more story to finish him off." She smiled. "And you can help me get it."

"Why do you want to 'finish him off'?" Frank asked.

"Because he deserves it," Cindy said bitterly. "He's built his fortunes on a lot of people's backs. Look what he's doing to Lisa Summer. Holding her hostage to a contract that could ruin her career."

"Maybe there's another reason," Frank said. "Maybe you're out to get Mort because he fired you."

"Yes, he fired me," Cindy admitted. "I was the best writer he ever had. Accused me of giving away his precious trade secrets. But this isn't about me. I want to stop him from hurting any more people. Are you interested in helping me?"

"I'm listening," Frank said, wanting to keep her talking.

"Good. I need to know everything that goes on on the set of *Total Annihilation*," Cindy said. "I've already got the office and house covered. So what do you say? Will you cover the set for me?"

"What's in it for me?" Frank asked, playing along.

Cindy rubbed her thumb and fingers together in a gesture that meant money. "Plenty," she said with a grin.

Cindy was about to say more when a noise made her jump and look over her shoulder. Frank heard it, too. It was coming from the other end of the garage, and it sounded like a chain rattling, Frank thought.

As Frank peered through the dim light in the direction of the sound, Cindy got back into the taxi. Stepping hard on the gas, the driver peeled out, heading straight for the exit and leaving Frank alone.

Frank heard the rattling sound again. Then three tough-looking guys emerged from the shadows, heading right toward Frank. One was carrying a long, thick chain that trailed noisily on the cement floor.

Another carried a metal pipe. As he came closer, he slapped the pipe against the palm of his hand and gave Frank a cold-blooded smile.

9 A Growling Guard

As the three thugs started to close in on Frank, his eyes darted from one to the other. There was no time to run. He'd have to hold his ground.

"You guys want something," he said firmly, hoping to scare them off.

"Hey, man. We just want to be friends, that's all," the guy with the chain said. "Right, Cal?"

"Yeah. Friends. Right, Eddie," Cal answered. "And maybe borrow some money." He gave out a high-pitched giggle. The others joined in the mock laughter.

"I don't think so," Frank said.

"Not very friendly, is he, Cal?" Eddie growled, whipping the chain on the concrete garage floor.

With those words, Frank prepared to fight. He moved his body into a defensive karate position, his arms up and out in front, his feet spread apart. Crouching slightly, he fixed his gaze on the guy with the chain but kept the others in sight in his peripheral vision.

The thugs each took one more step toward Frank. They were now dangerously close to him.

Suddenly an amplified voice echoed throughout the garage.

"This is the police!" the voice bellowed. "We've got you surrounded. You're all under arrest." Like cockroaches, the three thugs scattered, scrambling for the nearest exits.

As Frank took a deep breath of relief, Joe stepped out from behind the Hardys' van, a megaphone in his hand. "That should take care of them," he said proudly.

"Thanks, Joe," Frank said. "Just in the nick of time."

"It's a good thing I took a cab down here," Joe explained. "As soon as I came in, I saw what was happening, so I sneaked into the van for something to scare them with." He held up the megaphone. "Where'd you get this?"

"They gave it to me on the set," Frank answered. "Told me it was for crowd control. I guess it works!"

"It's been some day, hasn't it, Frank?"

"You can say that again," Frank agreed. "Let's head home before something else happens."

"So what did Cindy have to say?" Joe asked as he guided the van through the traffic.

"The usual," Frank said. He leaned his head

back on the seat. "She said she had Mort just where she wanted him and needed just one more story to finish him off."

"That almost sounds like a confession," Joe said. "Do you think Cindy's the copycat?

"I don't know, Joe," Frank said, sighing loudly. "We know she hates Mort. And she's made it clear that she's got an informant at the office so she could have known about those secret endings."

"She's too short to have climbed onto Mort's balcony at the party," Joe pointed out.

"But it could have been her accomplice who did that," Frank countered.

Joe pulled into the driveway in front of their house and stopped. He looked over at his brother.

"Something's bothering me, though," Frank continued. "Three of the stunts fit the copycat M.O. exactly. But then there's the smoke machine and the sandbag accident on the set. They throw our theory right out the window."

"Maybe, but we still have to consider it," Joe said. "The only film left to see is *End of the Road*. It's the only rerelease on Mort's list. I'll try to get a look at it as soon as I can."

"Good," Frank said. "And tomorrow we're going to find out exactly who sabotaged the smoke machine."

"You know, Frank, I'm getting worried," Joe said. "Mort will be back in a few days and if we don't have any answers for him, we're history."

"Yeah," Frank agreed. "And if we don't solve this case, M.T. Productions might be history, too!"

Even though it was Saturday, the boys got up early. There was a lot of work to be done. They ate a quick breakfast and went out to the van.

"Where to?" Joe asked as he slid in beside his brother.

"The set," Frank answered, putting the van into gear and pulling out of the driveway. They headed for the warehouse in lower Westchester. Joe had checked the typewriter sample he'd gotten from the office the night before, but it didn't match the note left in Mort's safe. Frank hoped they'd do better with the fingerprints on the smoke bottle.

There was a large padlock on the warehouse door, so Frank and Joe went to the rear of the building. The loading bay door was also pad-locked, but they found an open window within reach.

"So much for security," Frank commented as they climbed through the window.

Frank took Joe directly to the equipment room. "I have a theory," he said. "Somebody came in here either the night before the shoot or early that morning and took a smoke bottle from here." He pointed to the box with the three remaining smoke bottles in it. "Follow me."

Frank led Joe out onto the warehouse floor and to the staircase. Although they couldn't smell any

84

ammonia on the first floor, they did catch a whiff of it in the stairwell.

On the second floor, Frank stopped in the hallway. "Do you smell ammonia up here?" he asked.

Joe sniffed. "Nope."

"Me either," Frank said. "Okay, here's my theory: The equipment room is too public a place to spend any time in and not expect to be seen. Whoever switched the fluids probably did it somewhere else in this building. Maybe in one of the rooms on this floor. One with a bathroom or sink in it."

"So what do we do?" Joe asked.

"Sniff around," Frank said with a grin.

Sniffing like hounds, the boys went from room to room. In the last room on the left, they discovered that Frank's theory was right. One of the bathroom sinks had the distinct odor of ammonia. It was the bathroom in Lisa Summer's dressing room.

"All right!" Frank said. "Lisa's fingerprints will be all over the place. Now let's see if they're on the bottle." He carefully unwrapped the bottle, opened his fingerprinting kit, and began dusting for prints around the sink and on the bottle.

Ten minutes later the boys had the proof they were looking for. "So Lisa sabotaged the smoke machine," Joe said as he followed Frank out the room and back down the hallway.

"Yes," Frank said, jogging down the stairs to the

first floor. "But what does that tell us? Did she pull off all the other stunts?"

"She couldn't have," Joe said. "She was on the set with you when Mort's house was broken into." The boys stepped out into the bright sunlight.

"But Raymond Brown, her trainer, wasn't," Frank said. "He left at 9:30 in the morning and didn't get back to the set until about 12:30 in the afternoon."

"Three hours to get to Mort's house, break in, and get back to the set?" Joe asked skeptically.

"Well, let's find out," Frank said, starting the van. "Check your watch, Joe. Let's time the drive from here to Mort's house."

Frank pulled away from the warehouse and headed for the highway. About ninety minutes later, he was driving down the winding driveway to Mort's house.

"I'm not so sure you could get here this fast on a weekday when there'd be a lot more traffic," Frank said, checking his watch. "And you'd still have to get through the security system."

Joe took something out of the glove compartment, then hopped out of the van. "So let's find out how long that would take."

"Are you serious?" Frank said, somewhat surprised at his brother's suggestion.

"Why not?" Joe suggested, heading for the front door. "This way, we can also see if someone really could break in after watching *Blood in the Streets*."

"You think you can get through it?" Frank asked his brother as he climbed out of the van.

"Mort said this system was just like the one in the movie. I think I can get us through it," Joe said with conviction.

"Okay," Frank said. "What are we waiting for?"

The first challenge was getting in the front door and that meant cracking the computerized control panel. "Hmmm. This might not be so easy after all," Joe said. "In *Blood in the Streets*, Raven Blue knew the code to the front door. We don't."

"Well, I know it's eight letters beginning with a *p*," Frank told him.

Joe looked surprised. "How do you know that?"

"I was watching Mort when he punched in the code the other day," Frank explained.

"Eight letters beginning with a *p*," Joe thought out loud. "It could be almost anything, Frank."

"How about this?" Stepping up to the control panel, Frank punched in the letters P-R-I-N-C-E-S-S. The lock on the door immediately clicked open.

"I'm impressed," Joe said.

Frank grinned. "Now what?" he asked.

"The video cameras," Joe said. "We've got to avoid them. Watch me." He slowly pushed the door open just wide enough for him to fit through. Dropping to his hands and knees, he crawled inside. Frank followed, pulling the door closed behind him.

As the two boys huddled inside the doorway, Joe looked around and spotted a video camera mounted high up on the wall on the other side of the foyer.

"Okay. One video camera over there scanning the room." Joe checked his watch, counting off the seconds to himself. "When the camera reaches that point over there," he said, pointing to the far wall, "we make a run for the living room. We have three seconds. Ready?"

Frank nodded. "Ready."

Joe watched the camera until it was in the right position. "Go!"

The boys darted across the foyer and into the living room. "So far so good," Frank said when no alarm sounded.

The door to the den was on the far side of the living room. "Now the hard part," Joe said. "The laser beams. In the movie there were a bunch of them crisscrossing the room," he explained. "If we walk into one, we set off the alarm."

Joe pulled out a book of matches he'd taken from the glove compartment of the van. Dropping to his knees again, he lit the whole book, then quickly blew it out. As the smoke drifted across the floor it illuminated some of the laser beams. They were running across the room, about a foot and a half off the floor. "There they are, Frank."

"I see them. How do we get around them?" Frank asked.

"We don't," Joe said. "We go *under* them. Raven Blue was able to crawl on her stomach and make it through."

"If she could do it, we can do it," Frank reasoned. "Let's go."

Almost flat on their stomachs, the boys began to crawl across the floor. Staying as low as they could, they slowly made their way to the other side of the living room.

"That was tougher than it looked in the movie," Joe said as the two boys rested at the door to the den.

Frank chuckled, then checked his watch. "It took us about five minutes to get this far," he said. "What's next?"

Joe wiped the perspiration from his forehead. "In the movie, there were no lasers in the room with the safe," he said. "Just a trip wire on the painting that hides the safe."

"Great. Let's do it."

The boys got to their feet. Joe cautiously opened the door to the den, then carefully scanned the room for cameras. There were none. The brothers slipped inside and moved quickly to the wall safe.

"This shouldn't be too difficult," Joe told Frank. "There's a latch attached to the wall, held in place by the painting's frame. We just have to make sure the latch doesn't fall when we pull the painting away."

Locating the latch, Joe held it up with one

finger. Just as he was beginning to ease the painting away from the wall, a deep rumbling sound filled the room.

Slowly, the boys turned their heads.

Standing in the open door of the den was a large Doberman pinscher, its lips curled back from its sharp teeth in a menacing snarl.

10 Up in the Air

The boys froze. For a few seconds the only sound was the deep-throated growl of the attack dog.

"Go for the desk," Frank whispered finally, trying not to move his lips.

"What about the alarm?" Joe asked, still holding his finger on the latch.

"Forget it," Frank said. "We've got to move before we become this dog's lunch. On the count of three. One. Two. Three!"

As the boys bolted for the desk, the Doberman took off after them, barking savagely. Joe leaped onto the desktop, then grabbed Frank's arm to help him up faster.

The Doberman was right on Frank's heels, but Frank managed to scramble up in time to escape its sharp teeth. As Frank and Joe edged over to the far side of the desk, the dog stood on its hind legs with just its large front paws on the desk, barking

91

and snapping. Then he dropped down and began to circle, growling ferociously. Above the growl the boys could hear a loud ringing alarm.

"There was no dog in *Blood in the Streets*, Frank!" Joe said with panic in his voice.

"Yeah, well, there's one in this room," Frank said.

The dog continued to circle, occasionally charging the desk, then backing off.

"Nice doggy. Nice doggy," Joe kept saying.

"I don't think that's going to help," Frank said.

"You got a better idea?" Joe snapped.

"Yeah. We stay cool and wait for the security guards to get here."

With the dog barking and snarling any time the boys even breathed, the wait seemed endless. Finally, after five long minutes, two burly security guards burst into the room with their guns drawn.

"All right, you two! Off the desk, up against the wall, with your hands in the air," the taller of the two guards ordered. "Now!"

As the shorter guard clipped a leash to the Doberman's collar, Frank and Joe hopped down from the desk. The dog growled and strained at the leash.

"Boy, are we glad to see you," Frank said, his hands above his head. "We're not burglars. We work for Mr. Tannenberg."

"Sure. And I'm the tooth fairy," the tall guard said.

"No, really," Joe added. "Ask George Brandish. He'll tell you."

"George is off today," the guard told them. "Gone fishing. You'll have to do better than that."

"Look," Frank said. "We really do work for Mort. If you don't believe us, call him."

"Mort Tannenberg is out of town," the second guard said.

"We know that," Joe said. "I have his number in Jamaica. It's in my pocket."

As Joe reached into his pocket, the Doberman growled and lurched forward. The second guard pulled the leash back to keep the dog from getting at the boys.

Joe took a piece of paper from his pocket, handed it to the tall guard, and quickly raised his hands again. The dog continued to growl but stopped tugging at the leash.

"What do you think, Sam?" the first guard said. "Should we do it?"

"I don't know, Gus." The second guard sounded skeptical. "Our orders were to contact Tannenberg only in an extreme emergency."

"This *is* an extreme emergency!" Joe pleaded.

Gus eyed the boys. "Okay. But if this is a trick, I might just let Rover there chew on a bone—one of yours!"

"It's no trick, really," Frank insisted. "Just tell Mr. Tannenberg that we're Frank and Joe Hardy."

Gus picked up the receiver from the phone on

Mort's desk, checked the paper Joe gave him, and punched in the numbers.

"Yeah, hello," he said when the connection went through. "Mort Tannenberg, please." He looked down at Joe's note. "Suite 504 . . . Mr. Tannenberg? This is Gus Thompson from Sentry Security. Sorry to bother you, sir, but we just apprehended two boys trying to break into your safe. They say they work for you. Frank and Joe Hardy."

Gus listened for a moment, then held the receiver out to Frank. "He wants to talk to you."

Frank took the receiver. "Hello, Mr. Tannenberg. This is Frank Hardy."

"What on earth is going on there, Frank?" Mort demanded.

"If you call off your guards and their dog, I can explain everything," Frank said.

"Push the speaker button on the phone," Mort instructed.

Frank pushed the button and Mort's voice filled the room. "All right. You security guards can go. I'll take care of this from here. And take the dog with you."

Frank waited for the two security guards to leave, Rover in tow. "Listen, Mr. Tannenberg," he began. But Mort cut him off.

"No, you listen and listen carefully," Mort's voice crackled over the speaker. "I don't know what the heck you're doing breaking into my house when you're supposed to be looking for the guy who's out to get me. I have a scene coming up on Wednesday that's going to cost a fortune to shoot and I'm convinced this nut is going to try something. I want him caught before he gets the chance. Do I make myself clear?"

"Very clear," Frank said, raising his eyebrows at Joe.

"It's scene thirteen of *Total Annihilation*," Mort continued. "It takes place at the old Palace Opera House in Milton, on the west side of the Hudson River. Get over there and check it out. And keep an eye on it until I get back."

"But Mr. Tannenberg . . ."

"No buts," Mort interrupted again. "That's where he's going to strike next. I know it. So get over there."

Joe took the receiver from Frank and cleared his throat. "Excuse me, Mr. Tannenberg. Joe here. Just one question."

"What is it?" Mort said impatiently.

"When did you get the dog?" Joe asked.

"When do you think I got him?" Mort said, irritated by the question. "When my $10,000 security system and my two super sleuths failed me, that's when. Now get to work!"

Mort hung up.

"Well, he's not a happy camper," Frank said to his brother as he hung up the receiver.

"No kidding. So what now?"

Frank shrugged. "I guess we check out the opera house."

The boys were quiet most of the trip to Milton, about a three-hour drive from Bayport. They both knew that time was running out, and they were beginning to feel the pressure.

"So what did we learn from our break-in?" Frank asked, finally breaking the silence.

"Not to fool around with attack dogs?"

Frank laughed. "Right. *And* that it took us ninety minutes to get from the warehouse to Mort's house," he said. "Another fifteen minutes to get to the safe. And figure another fifteen minutes to get out and an hour and a half more to get back to the set."

"Three and a half hours," Joe figured.

"Yeah, on a weekend with no traffic." Frank shook his head. "Unless Raymond can fly, there's no way he could have done it. Even without a Doberman pinscher to greet him."

Joe looked disappointed. "So Lisa, maybe with Raymond's help, sabotaged the smoke machine. But neither one of them did the break-in. Where does that leave us?" he asked.

Frank shook his head in frustration. "With a lot of questions and not much time to answer them."

Three hours later, the boys pulled up in front of the Palace Opera House in Milton. From the outside, with the overgrown weeds crawling up its peeling painted walls, the old theater looked like it had been out of use for a long time. The front door was locked, but Frank quickly got them in.

Inside, the boys walked through a musty-smelling lobby to the main auditorium. The interior, although a little shabby, still looked impressive. Joe let out a low whistle. "This must have been quite a place once."

The spacious auditorium had about three hundred seats. In front of the stage with its drawn, plush velvet curtain was a full orchestra pit.

Joe glanced around. There was a large balcony flanked on both sides with rows of box seats.

As they walked down the center aisle toward the stage, Frank spotted the film crew's cables, lights, and scaffolds.

"Looks like M.T. Productions has already been here getting the place ready," Frank noted.

The boys walked up the side steps and onto the stage, which was filled with scenery to look like a medieval castle.

"Do you know what scene thirteen is like?" Joe asked his brother.

Frank nodded. "They gave me a copy of the script and I read it last night." He moved to the center of the stage and looked up to a series of catwalks high above the stage floor. "It's not much, Joe," Frank explained. "An audience filled with extras, a thirty-piece orchestra in the pit, five opera singers on stage, and Lisa shooting a rifle at a deranged chemical engineer swinging across the stage on a rope." He laughed and gave a shrug. "That's all."

"Terrific," Joe commented sarcastically.

"Mort might be right," Frank said. "If someone wanted to ruin him, this would be a good place to do it."

"So where do we start?"

Frank looked around. "Why don't you check out the balcony and box seats?" he suggested. "I'll start on the stage. Look for loose cables, unsecured lights, anything that could be sabotaged. Then we'll go up on the catwalk."

As Joe headed for the balcony, Frank began to look around the stage. The castle was made up of a number of tall flats and platforms. Frank checked behind each one of the flats to make sure it was properly anchored to the stage floor.

Up in the balcony, Joe carefully examined each light he found. Then he made his way to the box seats stage left, planning to do the same thing there. But just as he reached the first light, he was sure he saw something move in the box seats on the opposite side. Was someone there?

Down below Frank heard a sound. He looked up to the box seats and then over to Joe. The boys exchanged a look, then Frank pointed silently to the staircase. He quietly walked off the stage and moved briskly to the rear of the auditorium.

Joe knew he had to do something fast. There were several exits from the theater. He didn't want the unidentified visitor to escape. But what could he do from so far away? He noticed a cable attached to the catwalk high above center stage. The other end of the cable was wrapped around the box seat railing right next to him.

Joe untied the cable and twisted it around his arm. With both hands he gave it a hard tug to make sure it was secure. Then in one quick move, he mounted the railing and pushed off with all the leg strength he could muster.

The box seats loomed in front of him. As he swung to the other side of the auditorium, Joe lifted his legs, preparing to hoist himself over the wall of the box. But he miscalculated. Instead of going over the wall, Joe hit it. With the cable still wrapped around his arm, he desperately grabbed for the wall. But as he took hold of it, the wall itself broke away, and he fell ten feet toward the floor below.

Joe had to think fast. He'd never be able to swing back to the other side and he had no idea how long the cable could support his weight. He grabbed onto the edge of the exposed box seat floor with one hand. The momentum of the cable was throwing him even more off balance so he let go of the cable and latched onto the floor of the box with his other hand.

As the cable whipped away from him, Joe

gasped for breath. He'd stopped himself from falling, but now he had to use every bit of strength to climb to safety.

Sweat began to roll down his forehead. His hands were sweaty, too, and he felt his grip loosening. His legs were dangling in midair, his arms were fully extended, and only his slippery hands were keeping him from crashing to the auditorium seats far below.

11 Surprise Endings

In desperation, Joe tried to swing one of his legs onto the box seat floor. But his hands slipped again and he gasped for air. He knew he couldn't hold on much longer.

"Frank!" I need help!" Joe's voice echoed throughout the auditorium.

Just then Frank entered the auditorium. He was out of breath. When he saw Joe, his adrenaline started pumping again.

"Hang on, Joe," he yelled as he charged down the center aisle. He raced over to a large scaffold that was set up in front of the stage. With all his strength he pushed the shaky structure toward the box seats, trying to maneuver it directly under his brother.

Joe's palms were slicker than ever. He felt himself slide again until he was holding on only by his fingertips.

"I can't hang on any longer, Frank!" Joe cried out, and felt himself begin to fall.

With a last desperate push, Frank shoved the scaffold forward. He was just in time. Joe dropped about ten feet and landed with a thud on the platform on top of the scaffold.

"Are you all right, Joe?" Frank called out, his brother no longer in his sight.

Joe leaned his head over the top of the scaffold. "This is not my lucky day, Frank," he said in between deep breaths.

"Need help getting down?"

"I think I can make it." Carefully, Joe climbed down the scaffolding to the floor and sank into an orchestra seat.

Frank sat down beside his brother. "What were you trying to do, play Tarzan?" he said jokingly, relieved that Joe was safe.

"I would have made it, Frank, but that box seat wall just collapsed," Joe explained.

"Probably a breakaway wall," Frank said. "According to the script, there's a fight scene up there. One of the terrorists crashes through it and falls to the stage."

"Ha! Maybe I can get the job," Joe said with a wry smile. Still breathing heavily, he asked, "Did you get a look at our intruder? Whoever it was was gone before I crashed."

"No, but I did catch a glimpse of a blue car roaring out of the parking lot," Frank said. "The first three numbers on the license plate were 529."

"That should give us something to go on," Joe said as Frank helped him to his feet. "So what do we do now?"

"You don't look like you're in any condition to do anything, Joe," Frank said. "Let's call it a wrap for the day."

Back at home, Joe collapsed on his bed while Frank phoned in the information about the blue car to one of Mr. Hardy's friends at the police department.

"It's the weekend and we might have to wait a while for a computer match on that license plate," Frank reported as he hung up the phone and sat down on his own bed.

"You think that was the culprit sabotaging the set?" Joe asked, staring up at the ceiling.

"I don't know." Frank leaned back and tucked his hands behind his head.

Just then, there was a knock at the door. "Frank, Joe?" Aunt Gertrude called. "Chet's here to see you."

"Come on in," Joe called out.

The door opened and Aunt Gertrude walked in wearing a flowery summer dress and carrying a large bowl of green grapes. Chet was right behind her, munching on one of the grapes.

"Here you go, boys," Aunt Gertrude said, putting the bowl down on the night table between the two beds.

Joe pulled off a couple of grapes and popped them into his mouth. "Thanks, Aunt G."

"You're welcome," she said with a warm smile.

As Aunt Gertrude closed the door behind her, Chet sat down on the edge of Joe's bed. "Well, well," he said with a laugh. "So this is the way you two solve mysteries, lying on your backs."

"Give us a break, Chet," Joe said. "This is the first chance all week we've had to take a breather."

"Yeah, well it's been tough for me, too," Chet said. "I had to make a million phone calls to get the information you guys asked for the other day."

"Did you find out anything?" Frank asked.

"I sure did," Chet said proudly. "Mort Tannenberg had no insurance on his yacht. He dropped it six months ago."

Frank sat up, surprised. "What about the rest of his financial situation?" he asked.

"It's shaky, but no worse than it's ever been," Chet reported. "He's got some financial partners in Jamaica who always come through for him when he needs money."

"Well, that explains the Jamaica trip," Frank said. "I think we can safely rule out Mort as a suspect." Joe nodded in agreement.

"So who's left?" Chet asked eagerly.

"Just about everybody else," Frank said, letting out a long sigh and flopping back on his bed again.

* * *

104

Following Mort's instructions, the boys spent an uneventful Sunday keeping an eye on the opera house. Frank called Mort in Jamaica to report that nothing happened at the set. There were still many unanswered questions, and Joe was eager to get back to work at Mort's office where he hoped to get the answer to the most urgent question: What happened in the last scene of *End of the Road?*

When he arrived at the office Monday morning, Joe knew getting a chance to view the movie wasn't going to be easy. Danny had a lot of work waiting for him.

"Label those film cans on the floor there," Danny instructed Joe, "and then label these." He handed Joe another stack of cans and went back to doing some paperwork at his desk.

Joe knew there was a copy of *End of the Road* sitting right on the shelf above Danny's desk. All he had to do was get his hands on it and then find the time to watch it: one hour and twenty-five minutes—that was the running time on the press release that Sandy had given him. But how could he do it without Danny seeing him?

Later in the morning, Sid Renfield entered Danny's office. "Greetings, gentlemen," he said.

Danny looked up from his paperwork. "Hi, Sid. How can we help you?"

"I just spoke to Mort," Sid said, handing Danny a piece of paper. "He gave me a list of things he wants you to do."

As Danny read the list, his faced dropped. "He wants me to do all this?"

"By Wednesday," Sid added.

"He's crazy," Danny said, visibly angered. "I can't get this done."

"You'd better," Sid warned Danny. Then he left the room.

"I don't believe it," Danny huffed, tossing the paper on his desk. "I can't deal with this now. I really can't. I'm going to lunch. Get those labels done," he said to Joe. "I'll be back at one."

Danny grabbed his sports jacket and left, slamming the door behind him. Joe checked his watch and smiled. He'd gotten lucky. It was 11:30 now, and that gave him just enough time to watch *End of the Road.*

Joe slipped the cans off the shelf and grabbed the sandwich he'd brought from home. Then he sneaked into the projection room and turned on the projector. Unfortunately, there was no way to fast-forward the film on the projector. He unwrapped his sandwich and began to watch the film.

End of the Road was from the late 1950s, and it starred Mort's wife, Samantha. Two things surprised Joe. The movie ended five minutes earlier than it was supposed to according to the press release. The other thing he noticed was that the ending was not like the other films Joe had seen. No surprises. Just Samantha and her partner apprehending the bad guy and then driving off into the sunset. *Nothing to be worried about here,* Joe thought. Maybe the copycat theory was wrong after all. But something made him uneasy. The running time of each movie was clocked to the second. Why was this film five whole minutes off?

By the time Danny returned, Joe had placed *End of the Road* back on the shelf and was frantically trying to get all the labels finished.

"They're not done yet?" Danny almost shouted.

"Just five more minutes, Danny," Joe told him. "That's all I need."

"Well, move it. We've got a ton of things to do." Danny picked up the piece of paper that Sid had given him and shook his head in disgust.

"I'm getting really tired of Mort Tannenberg," he said to Joe. "You know whose idea the ending to *Blood in the Streets* was? Mine!"

"Really?" Joe asked.

"That's right," Danny went on. "When the script was being developed, I was the one who suggested that Raven Blue reach into the safe and get electrocuted. And did I get any credit for it? Not even a thank you."

Danny began to pace around the office. "You know, I didn't take this job to spend the rest of my life being an office boy. I'm a writer, not a techie. I took this job so I could show Mort my scripts. But he just doesn't take me seriously. I've already given him six scripts and he hasn't read one of them."

"That's too bad," Joe said sympathetically.

107

"Too bad? It's a *crime.*" Danny said, still pacing. "But he's going to get what he deserves! Count on it!"

Joe kept his expression sympathetic, but Danny's words made him wonder. Whatever Danny planned for Mort, could it be what he and Frank were looking for?

Finally Danny stopped pacing and went back to his desk. Fidgeting with a pencil, he picked up the phone and punched in some numbers. As he waited for his party to answer, he looked over to Joe.

"Joe. Take those cans and finish up your work in the projection room," he said, holding his hand over the phone's mouthpiece. "I'll be there in a few minutes."

Joe didn't have much choice, so he took the cans into the projection booth. It was pretty obvious that Danny didn't want him to hear his phone conversation. Was he talking to an accomplice who would help him "get" Mort?

When Danny joined Joe a few minutes later, he announced he had to run an errand and would be back shortly. Joe wasted no time. He raced back to Danny's office, picked up the phone, and punched the redial button.

The phone automatically dialed the last number dialed. Joe listened anxiously as it rang on the other end. Then someone picked up.

"The *Star Times.* Cindy Langly here," the voice said. Joe immediately hung up the phone.

108

Cindy Langly! So it was Danny who was Cindy's spy at the office. Maybe he was even more than that. Remembering that it was Danny he saw in the prop room his first day on the job, Joe wondered if Danny and Cindy were partners. Partners in crime!

Joe's thoughts were interrupted by a noise that made him jump. It sounded like a gunshot. Joe leaped up, then caught himself. Maybe he'd imagined it. Maybe it just was a car backfiring. Still, he had to check it out.

Crossing the small office, he opened the door and cautiously stuck his head out. Just as he did, a second shot rang out. That was no car.

His heart pounding, Joe shoved the door open wide and stepped into the hallway. That's when he heard a second sound—a loud thud.

A chill ran down Joe's spine. The thud he'd heard was the sound of a falling body.

12 A Deadly Plot Twist

Running down the hall as fast as he could, Joe heard two more shots ring out, followed by another body thudding to the floor. The sounds were coming from the audio studio.

About four feet from the studio, Joe stopped running and flattened himself against the wall. His heart hammering, he sidestepped cautiously to the door.

Taking a deep breath, Joe spun around the door frame and threw himself into the studio. The force of his entry made him land on the floor.

Startled, Sid Renfield and the audio engineer, Mack Clark, looked up from the mixing board. "Are you okay?" Clark asked Joe.

Joe looked around. There were no bodies. No blood. No killer. He looked back at the mixing board and suddenly realized that everything he'd heard had been on tape!

Joe got up quickly and tried to hide his embarrassment. "I was curious about the audio and I guess I just tripped." He gave a self-conscious laugh. "The track sounded good."

"Well, I'm still not happy. Something's wrong. Excuse me." Ignoring Joe, Sid nudged Mack from his chair and sat down in front of the tape machine. He manually rolled the tape back a little way. Then he shuttled it back and forth a moment.

Pulling the tape away from the tapehead, Sid pressed it into a splicing block mounted on the machine. Then he took a razor blade and slit the tape. Next, he located another spot and slit the tape there. He attached the two remaining loose ends with splicing tape. Then he spliced in the cutout piece there. Finally, he carefully rethreaded the tape back onto the machine.

"Listen to it this way," Sid said to the engineer, punching the button. Now the tape played: "Look out! He's got a gun!" Then the two gunshots.

Sid had reversed the lines. Joe was impressed. It really made a difference.

"Sounds much better," Mack said.

"Okay, let's keep going," Sid said. But before they could continue, the intercom buzzed.

"Sid, are you there?" Sandy's voice asked over the small speaker.

"What's up, Sandy?" Sid asked.

"Peter Rizer's here to see you."

Sid looked annoyed. "What does he want now?"

"Says he has to talk to you about Wednesday's

scene," Sandy said through the intercom. "And that it's really important."

"All right. Send him to my office, Sandy. I'll be right there." Sid stood up and went out the door.

Joe noticed the producer had left some papers behind and he quickly picked them up. "I'd better take these to Sid," he said to Mack. "Thanks for letting me sit in on the sweetening session."

"Anytime, Joe," the engineer said as he went back to editing tape.

Joe didn't really want to return Sid's papers. He wanted to listen in on the conversation with Peter. Quietly, he approached Sid's office. The door was closed, so Joe leaned his ear as close to it as possible. But he didn't get a chance to hear anything, because at that very moment, the door flew open and Joe almost fell into the room.

Peter, looking frustrated, strode out of the office and down the hall. Sid, sitting at his desk, glared at Joe.

"What were you doing listening in at my door?" Sid asked accusingly.

"I wasn't listening in, Mr. Renfield. Really," Joe said. "I just came to return these notes you left in the audio studio," he said as he held them out.

Sid grabbed the papers, then gave Joe another suspicious look. "Thanks," he said gruffly.

As he left, Joe let out a sigh of relief. It was a good thing he'd had the papers as an excuse.

* * *

112

"I don't know if Sid believed me or not," Joe told Frank later that evening. The boys were sitting in the kitchen after dinner, discussing the day's events.

"Well, check this out," Frank said, handing his brother a fax. "It's a list of license plate numbers from the police department, and guess whose is on it?"

Joe scanned the two-page list. Near the bottom of the second page, he saw a familiar name. "Cindy Langly!" he said. "It figures."

"What do you mean?" Frank asked.

"Oh, right, I didn't tell you yet," Joe said. "At the office today, Danny was really angry at Mort. Said he'd get what he deserved. And then he made a call to none other than Cindy Langly."

"You're kidding! What did they talk about?"

"I didn't hear the conversation," Joe said. "And then I got distracted by two gunshots."

"What?" Frank asked, stunned.

Joe laughed. "It was nothing. Just some audio sweetening," he said. "Sid and the engineer were putting together some sound effects. You know, Frank, you can do almost anything with audio tape. They didn't like the sequence of lines, so Sid just sliced the tape up, rearranged it, and put it back together again."

What Joe had just described got Frank to thinking, and he sat in silence for a moment. Then he said, "What if that's the way Samantha's voice was done the night Mort was haunted?"

113

"You mean someone got a bunch of tapes of her voice and edited them together?" Joe asked.

"Right. That way, they could make Samantha say anything." Frank frowned. "But how could someone get tapes of her voice?"

"That's easy," Joe said. "From the soundtracks of her old movies. And what's more, by splicing the tapes they wouldn't have to use a real line from a movie. That way Mort wouldn't recognize it."

Frank thought for a few more moments. Then he jumped up. "That's it!" he said, snapping his fingers. "Come on, Joe. We're going back to Mort's house. I need to check that answering machine again."

A short while later the boys were driving down the narrow beach-front road that led to Mort's house. Joe suddenly remembered something. "Frank," he exclaimed. "What about Rover?"

Before Frank could answer, he noticed a Jeep that seemed to be following them. By the time Frank pulled the van into Mort's driveway, the Jeep was gone. *I must just be on edge,* Frank thought.

At the front door to the house, Joe was surprised that Frank didn't use the access code. He just rang the doorbell.

"You expecting Rover to answer the door?" he asked.

"You'll see," Frank said with a big smile.

"Greetings and salutations!" Chet said as he

opened the door. In his hand was a large bowl of ice cream.

"Chet! What are you doing here?" Joe asked in surprise.

"House-sitting," Chet said. "Frank thought it would be a good idea. And Mort agreed."

"I thought of it when I checked in with him on Sunday," Frank explained.

Joe smiled as they entered the house. "You're a much better host than Rover," he joked.

In Mort's bedroom, Frank went straight to the answering machine. "The other night I pressed the Messages button, and I expected to hear Samantha's voice," he said. "But what if someone used the phone's *outgoing* message tape instead? The one you'd hear if you called Mort," he explained. Reaching down, he popped the outgoing message tape from the machine. "What if somebody then reprogrammed it?" he went on. "If they did, there just might be some of Samantha's voice left on the end of this tape."

"I'm confused," Chet said through a mouthful of ice cream.

"Come on," Frank said, leading the way to Mort's den. "We'll need to play the tape in a regular cassette player to get past the first message."

In the den, Frank turned on the stereo and inserted the tape into the system's cassette player. Then he pushed Play.

115

First came Mort's normal message, then a clicking sound. After a few seconds of silence, the boys heard the remainder of another message. "Come in, honey," a woman's voice said. It was the same voice Frank had heard the night of the haunting. The one Mort was certain belonged to Samantha.

"Bingo!" Joe said.

"I'm still confused," Chet said. "What's going on?"

"It looks like somebody made a tape of Mort's wife's voice and put it on the outgoing message tape," Frank explained. "Then all they had to do was play it at the right moment. The beauty of the whole thing is that it could all be done by remote."

"Right," Joe said. "You just call up and punch in the answering machine's access code to get beyond the regular message to a second one. Very clever."

"Well, I give up," Chet said. "I still don't know what you guys are talking about."

Sinking into the black leather couch, Chet scraped the last of the ice cream out of the bowl, grabbed the remote control, and flipped on the large-screen TV. A tag-team wrestling match came on the air.

"Wrestling. Cool," Chet said. Then he noticed that the Hardys were leaving. "Hey, where are you guys going?" he asked. "It's the Bash Brothers versus Killer Crawford and Mario Mendez. Should be a neat fight."

"No thanks, Chet," Joe called back. "There's

enough fighting around M.T. Productions for us. See you."

Chet just waved, his eyes focused on the wrestling match.

Outside, Frank and Joe got into their van and pulled out of Mort's driveway. They were heading back up the beach access road when suddenly they heard a loud popping sound. The van swerved sharply to the left.

"I think we've got a flat!" Frank yelled, maneuvering to keep control of the van.

"Doesn't surprise me!" Joe said as he held on. "Nothing surprises me anymore."

After a moment, Frank brought the van to a safe stop on the side of the road and turned the engine off. The boys climbed out to examine the damage.

"It's a flat, all right," Joe said as he pulled a large nail from the front left tire. Then he went to the rear of the van, opened the back doors, and pulled out a jack and spare tire.

It was dark by now, and Frank held a flashlight as Joe attached the jack. Joe was almost finished when they saw the headlights of an approaching car.

Looking up, Frank saw that it was moving very fast. "Watch out, Joe!" he yelled. Joe looked up and pressed himself against the van.

Its engine rumbling, the car raced right by the van, barely missing it. Up close, Frank could see that it was a Jeep.

117

"Another lunatic driver," Joe commented, then went back to the jack and started cranking it again.

Frank frowned. Was that the same Jeep he'd seen following them before?

Suddenly, with an ear-piercing squeal of brakes, the Jeep made a U-turn and revved its engine. Frank saw the Jeep heading back down the road at full speed, the glare from the headlights blinding him. There was no doubt—it was heading straight for them!

13 A Chilling Experience

"He's going to hit us!" Frank shouted. "Come on!"

Frank and Joe dove off the access road and onto the sandy beach next to it. They watched as the Jeep zoomed past the van.

"What's going on?" Joe asked.

"I don't know," Frank said, keeping his eyes on the Jeep. It made another U-turn and headed for the van again. Then it did something that surprised both boys. It turned onto the beach right where the brothers were standing.

"Let's get out of here fast!" Frank said, and the two boys began to run. The beach was dark and full of dunes, but the boys were lit up like jack rabbits by the headlights of the on-coming Jeep.

"This way!" Frank yelled to his brother, and they made a sharp right turn and jumped into a dune, rolling over in the sand. The Jeep turned quickly and came after them.

Joe was right with him. "Why is he after us?" he asked, breathing heavily.

"Let's figure that out later!" Frank panted.

The boys continued to run, zigzagging through the dunes, trying to keep ahead of the Jeep. But it stayed dangerously close, driving in and out of the dunes in hot pursuit.

There was no way the boys could outrun the Jeep and Frank knew it. "Okay," he yelled to Joe as they ran, "I've got a plan."

"It better be a good one," Joe gasped.

"Let's split up. You go left, I'll go right," Frank said. "Head for the water. We'll meet there."

"Got it," Joe said as he bolted to his left, then raced full speed for the bay.

Its engine roaring, the Jeep went after Joe. Joe didn't look back. He just kept zigzagging, running as fast as he could over the sand. The shoreline was only about twenty feet away, but he could hear the Jeep closing in on him. Putting on one last burst of speed, Joe made it to the water and ran in.

Brakes squealing, the Jeep veered sharply at the water's edge. Joe started swimming, still not looking back. The water was freezing cold, but he kept going until he knew he was a safe distance from shore.

Breathless, Joe treaded water for a few minutes, looking back to the beach, then out into the water. He could no longer see the Jeep or his brother.

Finally he heard Frank's voice calling to him across the water.

"I'm over here, Frank!" Joe called back.

Guided by their voices, the boys started swimming toward each other in the darkness. "That was close," Frank said as he reached Joe.

"Too close!" Joe said.

"The person or people must have been around Mort's place and saw us arrive or else the Jeep followed us all the way from home," Frank said. "Maybe we're closer than we think on this case, and the culprit's worried. Come on, let's get out of here before the Jeep comes back."

Still breathing heavily, the two boys swam back to shore, raced to the van, and fixed the flat. They managed to make it home safely without further incident.

The following morning, as Joe was getting ready to go to the office, Frank suggested he take their father's car instead of the train. "Things are heating up," he said. "We both have to be ready to move quickly."

Joe agreed and an hour or so later parked his father's car in the building's underground garage, then rode the elevator to the ninth floor. The M.T. Productions offices were buzzing with activity. Danny, Sid, and Paul were all there, and even Lisa and Raymond had dropped by. As far as Joe was concerned, any one of them could have been sitting behind the wheel of that Jeep last night.

Danny was his usual angry self, still complaining about all the work he had to do.

"Before you do anything, go down to a video store and rent these movies for Mort," Danny ordered, handing Joe a piece of paper. "He's thinking of remaking some old westerns and he wants them here when he gets back. You can get petty cash from Sandy."

Joe located a video store four blocks from the studio and found a copy of each movie. The cover of the fourth one had a label pasted across it: First Release with Original Ending.

As Joe returned to Danny's office, two words kept running through his mind: *Original ending.* Could *End of the Road* have had a different ending? That would explain the disparity in the running time. And if there *was* another ending, maybe it would be more like the other films Mort was releasing, Joe thought. Maybe it had a violent surprise ending, one that just might help him and Frank decide if the copycat theory made any sense at all.

Joe knew where he could find the answer: in the film vault. If another ending did exist, it would be there, sitting on a shelf.

Joe also knew that the only way he was going to get into the locked vault was with Danny. He had to be ready. While Danny was busy on the phone, Joe took a roll of gaffer's tape—electrician's tape, used on film sets in all sorts of emergencies—and cut off a small piece. He attached the tape to his belt and concealed it under his T-shirt.

Joe didn't have to wait long for a chance to put

his plan into action. When Danny got off the phone, he noticed a piece of paper on his desk. "Oh, great!" he said in exasperation. "I forgot to get these films for Sid. He's going to blow a gasket. Come on, I'm going to need your help."

Joe eagerly followed Danny to the vault. Once inside, Danny scanned the list. Then he started taking film cans off the shelves and handing them to Joe. He never went to the back of the vault, so there was no way Joe could see if an alternate reel to *End of the Road* was there.

Danny stacked seven cans in Joe's outstretched arms. They went up to his chin. "That should do it," Danny said. He walked to the door and held it open.

When Joe reached the doorway he deliberately dropped the top film can, making it look like an accident.

"Can't you do anything right?" Danny yelled.

As Danny reached down to pick up the can that had rolled into the hallway, he let go of the door. With his body shielding him from Danny's view, Joe quickly pulled the tape from his belt and attached it to the doorjamb, right over the locking bolt. Then he let the door slam shut.

Joe had finished just in time. Danny stood up and shoved the can he'd picked up against Joe's chest.

"Here. See if you can hold on to it this time," he snarled.

"Sorry," Joe said.

Danny took Sid's list and placed it on top of the pile. Joe clamped it in place with his chin. "Now, go deliver this stuff to Sid," Danny instructed Joe. Then he headed back to his office.

Joe found Sid's office locked as usual, so he went to the screening room. Sid was in conference with a few editors. Joe put the film cans down on a chair but pocketed the list. He had noticed that Sid had typed the note. It would be a good sample to compare to the cryptic note found in Mort's safe.

Joe wanted to stick around and see what information he could pick up, but before he could, Sid noticed him.

"Anything I can do for you, Joe?" he asked sharply.

"No. Nothing," Joe replied. "I'm just delivering the films you asked for the other day."

"Well, it's about time. I thought Danny had forgotten about me," Sid said.

Joe made his way back to Danny's office. If the gaffer's tape worked, then he could get back into the vault anytime he wanted to. That time came when Danny left for lunch.

There were still people in their offices, but Joe had to take the chance. If Danny came back from lunch and discovered the tape on his next trip to the vault, Joe knew he'd be the one Danny would suspect.

Cautiously, Joe peered out of Danny's office. No one was in the hallway. *It's now or never,* he said to himself. He walked briskly to the film vault door and pulled on the doorknob. The tape trick had worked, because the door opened. He slipped inside, pushing the door closed as quietly as he could.

Joe moved quickly to the rear of the vault to Mort's private collection and began to search the shelves for the film cans marked *End of the Road*. Finally he located them and found what he was looking for: a can marked *End of the Road— Alternate Ending*. "Bingo," Joe said softly.

As Joe was pulling the can off the shelf, he heard a noise at the door to the vault. He crouched down and hid behind one of the metal shelves. Was someone at the door? Had Danny come back early from lunch?

After a few minutes of silence, Joe decided the coast was clear. With the film can tucked under his arm, he headed for the door. But when he tried to open it, he found it locked. On the floor at his feet he noticed the tape he had used to keep the door open. Someone had taken it off.

Joe was locked inside the vault.

14 Time's Running Out

I'm in big trouble now, Joe thought as he stood behind the locked door. He could just start pounding, blow his cover, and maybe find himself face-to-face with the culprit, whom he suspected had locked him in there. Or he could wait until someone came in, which might not be for days.

Joe looked around the vault and spotted an air vent on the ceiling. It was large enough for a person to fit through.

Joe took the film can labeled *End of the Road— Alternate Ending* and climbed up the metal shelves to reach the vent. Using his pocketknife, he loosened the four screws that held the vent's grille in place. Then he pulled hard on the grille. It popped off, and he set it down on the top shelf.

The air duct was about three feet wide by two and a half feet high. Joe peered inside and saw that it was pitch black. *It's the only way out,* he thought, trying to convince himself. He placed the film can inside the duct, then hoisted himself up.

Lying flat on his stomach, Joe looked down the duct and saw only total darkness. Maybe this hadn't been such a good idea after all.

Despite his second thoughts, Joe decided to press on. Knowing he had to be very quiet because he'd be moving right over offices, he put the film can on his back and held it in place with his hand and lower arm. It was awkward, but it was the best he could do to keep the can from knocking against the metal duct.

Joe took a deep breath, then started to crawl. Pulling with his free hand, pushing with his feet, he headed down the dark air duct hoping to find Danny's office.

About twenty feet into the duct, Joe reached what appeared to be a cross section that went left and right. He could see light in both directions. Choosing to go left, Joe twisted his body around the bend in the duct. He didn't think the first light would be Danny's office, but it was in the right direction.

Joe crawled slowly, trying to be extra quiet as he approached the vent. He moved up to it and peeked through the grille into the room below. It was the screening room. He could see Sid and Peter Rizer seated in the first row, talking.

"It's been a nightmare," Peter was saying. "But it hasn't been all my fault, really."

"If you're looking for sympathy," Sid said,

"you've got the wrong guy. Production is your headache now, not mine. I need to get going. I'll be out of the office the rest of the day." Sid stood up to leave, but Peter grabbed his arm.

"Come on, Sid," Peter pleaded. "All I'm asking for is some advice."

"Okay, Peter," Sid responded, pushing Peter's hand away. "In this business you either deliver or you're history. So my advice is, you'd better deliver."

"Is that what happened to you?" Peter asked. "You couldn't deliver, so Mort kicked you upstairs?"

"Hey, anything between me and Mort is none of your business," Sid snapped.

Interesting, Joe thought. *Maybe Sid and Mort aren't such good friends after all.*

As Sid turned to leave, the film can slipped from Joe's sweaty hand and hit the duct with a loud, metallic clang. He quickly jerked his head away from the vent.

"What was that?" Joe heard Sid say from the room below. "It sounded like it came from . . ."

Before Sid could finish the sentence, a loud clicking sound echoed throughout the duct. Then a blast of ice-cold air hit Joe in the face.

"Just the air-conditioning," Paul said, and the two men left the room.

Relieved, Joe wiped the sweat from his hands, carefully readjusted the film can, and began to crawl again. He was getting very cold. The icy air was blowing directly into his face. His eyes were tearing and his hands were becoming numb. Joe knew he had to find an empty office—fast!

As rapidly as he could, Joe crawled down the duct until he came to the next shaft of light. Shivering from the cold, he inched his way along the duct until he made his way to the next vent. Looking down, he breathed a frosty sigh of relief. He was right over Danny's office. And he was in luck. Danny seemed to still be at lunch.

Joe reached into his pocket for his knife, but his fingers were so numb that he couldn't move them. It didn't matter—he soon discovered that the screws holding the vent's grille in place were on the other side!

Now what? Joe wondered, feeling like a jerk. He thought for a moment, then slipped the film can off his back and set it down in the duct. Rolling over onto his back, he positioned his feet directly on top of the grille. Then he lifted his feet as high as he could and with all his strength slammed them down onto the grille.

The grille didn't seem to budge. *Terrific,* Joe thought. *What a way to spend a lunch break!* Taking a deep breath, he tried again. This time when his feet hit the grille, it popped off and crashed to the floor in Danny's office.

Yesss! Joe said to himself. He grabbed the film can and dropped down into the office. He hoped no one had heard the noise. Still shivering, he checked his watch. It was 12:35. It was going to be tight, but he thought he had just enough time to view the film before Danny came back.

Joe hid the grille behind his desk, then sneaked into the projection booth and peeked through the glass window into the adjoining room. It was empty.

Working fast, Joe quickly threaded the projector with *End of the Road*—Alternate Ending. Once again he wished there was some way to fast-forward on the projector. He turned off all the lights and speakers, plugged a headset into the control panel, and slipped it on his head. *This better be worth it,* he thought as he started up the projector.

Most of the alternate scene was exactly like the other one Joe had seen. But at the part where Samantha and her partner captured the bad guy, the action began to change.

"You won't get away with this!" the bad guy called out as the police hauled him away. "I'll get my sweet revenge. You can be sure of that!" Those lines were not in the other version, Joe remembered.

Samantha and her partner got into a black sedan and drove off. *That's the same,* Joe thought. But then, instead of the car riding off into the sunset, it began driving down the side of a mountain. And there was more dialogue inside the car—dialogue that revealed that it was Samantha and her partner who had committed the crimes. They even joked

130

about it. *This is a cool twist to the story,* Joe thought.

But then Joe saw the real shocker.

It began with a close-up of Samantha's foot pumping the brake pedal. Then she yelled out that the brakes weren't working. She desperately tried to control the car as it picked up speed. A steep cliff was to her right, the mountain to her left.

"It was Tom," she cried, terror showing on her face. "He cut the brake line!"

The car careened back and forth across the road. More close-ups of Samantha pumping the brake pedal followed. Joe held his breath. Then his mouth dropped open. The car went over the cliff. Joe watched in horror as it flew through the air and crashed, bursting into a ball of fire at the base of the mountain.

"Wow!" Joe said out loud. Could this be the next copycat crime? The final and *fatal* one for Mort Tannenberg?

Quickly rewinding the film, Joe pulled it off the projector and put it back into the metal can. Just as he finished, the projection booth door opened and Danny stepped in. "What are you doing in here?" he demanded.

Joe had to think fast. He reached out to the projector and popped open the door that housed the projection lamp. "Oh, I just came in here to change the bulb on the projector," he said. "It blew earlier."

131

"Well, move it," Danny said angrily. "I've got a ton of stuff for you to do."

Sorry, Danny, Joe thought as Danny left the room. *I've got more important things to do.* He punched in the number for the Palace Opera House, which his brother was guarding as Mort had ordered.

Come on, Frank, Joe urged silently as the phone began to ring. *Pick it up.*

Finally Frank answered. "Hello."

"Frank! Frank!" Joe said in an excited whisper. *"End of the Road* has an alternate ending—the one I think Mort plans to use for the rerelease. And guess what?"

"What?" Frank asked.

"Murder, Frank. Murder! And it follows the pattern of all the other copycat crimes," Joe said. "But I can't talk now. I'll meet you as soon as I can at the opera house. And be careful," he added.

"You, too, Joe. See you later."

Frank hung up, and just as Joe was about to do the same, he heard a clicking sound on the telephone line. Was someone listening in on the conversation? He decided not to take any chances and left the office immediately. He wanted to get to his brother as fast as he could.

At the opera house, Frank was excited about Joe's news. If the copycat crimes were the M.O., he thought, then the field of suspects was narrowed. Mort would be back from Jamaica in a few hours and Frank hoped by then they could have some answers for him.

Walking back to the stage, Frank sat down next to a stack of the *Star Times* that Chet had given him. He read Cindy Langly articles, thought about the case, and waited anxiously for Joe to arrive.

Shortly after 5:00 P.M., Joe came running into the theater. "Boy, Frank," he said excitedly, "do I have things to tell you!"

But Joe didn't have the chance to tell Frank anything. As soon as he joined his brother on stage, the tall flat behind them began to wobble.

"Look out!" Frank shouted.

But Frank's warning was too late. There was no way the boys could move fast enough, and with a creaking, splintering sound, the heavy flat came crashing down on top of them.

15 The Final Cut

The flat hit the boys hard, knocking them to the stage floor. For a moment, both boys lay motionless, covered with splintered pieces of wood and ripped canvas.

Finally, Frank coughed and started pushing the debris off his body. A canvas section had fallen on him, and he was uninjured. Still a little stunned, he got to his feet.

"Joe? You okay?" he called out. Joe didn't answer. Frank frantically began to pull pieces of wood from the general area where Joe had been standing before the wall fell.

Frank found his brother beneath the rubble, face down on the floor, a piece of a two-by-four next to his head.

"Joe!" Frank kneeled down beside his motionless brother. "Are you okay?" Still no response. Frank leaned close, putting his hand on Joe's back.

134

After a second, he felt his brother's back rise and fall. *He's breathing*, Frank thought in relief.

"Joe," Frank said again, gently shaking Joe's shoulder.

Joe slowly began to move his head. Then he opened his eyes. "Frank? What happened?" he said, barely audible.

"The flat fell on us."

"Oh," Joe said. "It felt like a whole house."

"Does anything feel broken? Any pain anywhere?" Frank asked anxiously.

With Frank's help, Joe gingerly rolled onto his back. As he did, he put his hand on his head and winced in pain. "Just my head."

Frank smiled. "Well, you've always had a hard head," he said. "Let's try to get you up so we can get out of here, okay?"

"Okay."

It took a few minutes, but Frank was finally able to get Joe on his feet. Joe was very wobbly and kept a tight hold of his brother's arm.

"Do you think this was just an accident, Frank?"

"No way," Frank said firmly. "I checked that wall three times."

"But who knew we were here?" Joe said, taking a few slow steps.

"Probably the same person who was driving that Jeep the other night," Frank said. "Or the blue car the other day."

Joe stopped and looked at his brother. "Who do you think is on to us?"

135

Before Frank could answer, the boys heard a door at the back of the auditorium slam shut. Frank quickly eased Joe back down on the stage floor and got ready for action. Was the copycat criminal coming back to finish them off?

But it was only Mort, tan from the Jamaica sun. As he came charging down the aisle, the first thing he saw was the toppled flat.

"My set!" he bellowed as he approached the stage. "What's happened to my set? It's ruined!"

"Someone pushed a flat on us," Frank said as Mort climbed the stairs to the stage.

"What did I tell you?" Mort yelled. "They're out to destroy me!" He stormed around the stage, kicking at the debris. Finally, Mort noticed Joe sitting on the stage floor, holding his head in his hands.

"What happened to him?" Mort asked Frank.

"I just told you," Frank said, not bothering to keep the anger out of his voice. "Someone pushed the flat on us and a piece of the wood hit Joe in the head. He might have a concussion."

"I'm okay," Joe said shakily. But it was obvious to Frank that he wasn't.

"I can't believe you guys let this happen right under your noses," Mort griped, clearly more concerned with his own problems than with Joe's injury. "We start shooting tomorrow morning, and if this set isn't rebuilt by then, I'm finished!"

Mort stormed off into the wings and got on the

phone. As Frank helped Joe up again, he could hear the producer shouting.

"I don't care what time it is, Sandy," Mort yelled. "Get every available person you can up here to help rebuild the set. Now!"

With Frank helping Joe, the brothers slowly began to walk off the stage. Just as they reached the center aisle, Mort stuck his head out from the wings. "Where do you think you're going?" he demanded.

"Home," Frank answered firmly. With one arm around Joe's waist, he helped his brother up the aisle and out of the theater.

In the van, Joe dozed off almost immediately. Once they got home, Aunt Gertrude took one look at Joe and helped Frank put him to bed.

"I'm fine," Joe reassured her as he lay down. "I'm just bruised." The boys finally convinced Gertrude that Joe was really okay and that it wasn't necessary to call their parents in Paris or to take him to the doctor. She gave Joe one last concerned look and then left the bedroom.

Almost immediately Joe fell into a fitful sleep. Frank could hear his brother muttering, "No brakes. Tom did it. No brakes."

Who is Tom? Frank wondered. He was glad his brother seemed to be all right but frustrated that he couldn't talk to him about the day's events.

Frank set his alarm for 4:30 A.M. and then lay down, mulling over the case. *We must be very close,* he figured. Otherwise the culprit wouldn't have tried to eliminate them. But *who* could it be? They had suspects with motives but no opportunity, suspects with opportunity but no motive—not to mention the necessary skill and information to pull off the copycat crimes.

This is getting me nowhere, Frank thought, disgusted. He got up, grabbed a pile of Cindy Langly articles, and plopped back down on his bed.

He must have dozed off while he was reading, because when the alarm went off, copies of the *Star Times* were scattered on the floor around his bed.

Frank shut off the alarm and went over to his brother. "Joe. Joe," Frank said, shaking his shoulder. "Can you get up?"

As Joe's eyes opened, he reached a hand to his head. "Ouch!" he said, wincing as his fingers touched a large bump.

"Are you in any shape to go to the opera house?" Frank asked.

"What time is it?" Joe asked, blinking sleepily.

"4:30," Frank told him. "A.M."

Joe groaned and rolled onto his stomach, burying his aching head in his pillow.

"The call time for the crew is seven," Frank reminded his brother. "Maybe I should go without you."

Joe rolled back over and sat up. "No way!" he said. "Not even a herd of wild buffalo could stop me from being there."

Even though he was eager to go, Joe had to drag his aching body out of bed, and when he did, he could barely get dressed. As he began to put on the jeans he'd worn the day before, he felt a piece of paper in the pocket.

"Hey, I almost forgot this," he said.

"What is it?" Frank asked, one foot already out the door.

"A typewriter sample."

"Bring it," Frank said. "You can take a look at it in the van."

The boys had a long drive ahead of them. "What happened yesterday?" Frank asked. "When you called me at the opera house yesterday, you said 'murder.' What did you mean? And who's Tom?"

"Tom?" Joe thought for a moment. "Oh, him. He's a character in *End of the Road.* One of the bad guys." Suddenly he realized he hadn't been able to tell Frank anything he had learned the day before.

"You won't believe what happened yesterday, Frank," Joe said. And for the rest of the drive Joe detailed the events. He began with his journey through the air duct after being locked in the film vault, told what he'd heard Sid and Paul talking about, and finished by describing the last scene to the alternate ending of *End of the Road.*

As Frank paid the toll at the last leg of their trip, Joe took the note from his pocket and began to compare it to the one they'd found in Mort's safe. He speculated aloud about the case.

"I think we're right about the copycat M.O., Frank," he said as he used a magnifying glass to compare the letters.

"But then how do the smoke machine and the other accidents on the set fit in?" Frank asked.

Joe sighed.

"I might have an answer," Frank added.

"What?" Joe looked up from his magnifying glass, his curiosity aroused.

"Okay, follow this," Frank began as they crossed the bridge to the other side of the Hudson River. "We know by the fingerprints that Lisa pulled off the smoke stunt."

"Right."

"And we know Lisa's motive. She wants out of her contract."

"Right again," Joe answered.

"I think Mort's cost-cutting and Peter Rizer's incompetence led to all the other accidents on the set," Frank said. "And it gave Lisa the idea to create her own 'accident.'"

"So what are you getting at?" Joe asked.

"I'm saying, let's forget about all the accidents on the set, *including* the smoke machine."

"Okay."

"Then what does that leave us with?" Frank asked.

"The yacht. The haunting. And the break-in." Joe counted them off on his fingers beginning with his index finger. Then he grabbed his pinkie.

"And the car crash!" he said excitedly. "From the *End of the Road!*"

"Exactly!" Frank said, turning off the highway and heading into the town of Milton. "And there's more," he went on. "Something I found that fits in with what you've been telling me."

As Frank kept talking, Joe went back to examining the typewriter sample. "There was a Cindy Langly story published last year," Frank said, "and the headline read: 'Executive Producer Gets Grade B Treatment from M.T.' It was about a certain guy whom Mort had dumped on after he had worked with him for thirty years."

Before Frank could finish, Joe practically jumped out of his seat. "It's a match! It's a match!" he shouted, holding the note up.

"And it's from Sid Renfield's typewriter, isn't it?" Frank said.

Joe stared at him in surprise. "Yes. But how did *you* know?"

"Because that's who Cindy's article was about," Frank said. "Sid Renfield."

"But Sid is still with Mort. And he's handling the rereleases. That's a big job," Joe protested.

"That was what the article was about," Frank explained. "It just seems like a big job, but it's really a step down. It was like a cop being taken off active duty and stuck behind a desk."

"It makes sense as a motive, Frank," Joe said excitedly. "Not only does he get taken off the production stuff but Peter Rizer, a kid fresh out of film school, is handling his old job. After thirty years, that's got to hurt."

"Finally!" Frank exclaimed with satisfaction. "We have a suspect who has a motive *and* the know-how to pull off the crimes."

16 The End of the Road

If Sid Renfield was going to stick to his M.O., then Joe was almost certain that he wouldn't try anything during the shoot. Sid would save his "final cut" for later, when Mort was driving home down the winding mountain road.

With their minds on catching Sid Renfield, the boys weren't prepared for what they saw when they entered the auditorium. "Wow!" Frank exclaimed. "Look at this place!"

Hundreds of costumed extras were milling about. Musicians in tuxedos were tuning up in the orchestra pit. The place had been transformed from a run-down theater into the bustling, shining opera house it had once been.

The boys also noticed that Mort had hired two uniformed security guards and one of them was built like a Mack truck.

The flat and the box seat wall that had crumbled had been repaired. Mort was pacing, Peter Rizer was yelling, and Sid was standing in the wings, looking a little nervous.

"Further proof we've found our culprit," Frank said to his brother in a low voice. "He's not usually on the set anymore."

"Yeah," Joe added, "but who's going to stop him."

"We still have a few loose ends to tie up, Joe," Frank whispered to his brother. "Like Lisa."

Joe looked puzzled. "But I thought . . ."

"I know," Frank interrupted. "But we can't be too careful. She might have some new stunt planned. After all, she still wants out of her contract."

"Right," Joe agreed. "How do we keep her from messing things up?"

"I think I know," Frank said as he spotted Raymond Brown, Lisa's trainer, heading up the aisle toward the dressing rooms. "Stay here," he told Joe. "I'll be right back."

"Raymond!" Frank called, catching up to the stunt coach. "Got a second?"

"Hey, Frank. How you doing?" Raymond asked with a friendly smile. "Big scene today, huh?"

"Right, the money shot," Frank said. "But listen," he added, pulling Raymond aside, "I've got to talk to you about something serious."

"Sure. What's up, Frank?"

Frank didn't waste any time. "Look, I know about the smoke machine."

Raymond's face went blank. "What are you talking about?"

"You know what I'm talking about," Frank said firmly. "Lisa's fingerprints were all over the smoke bottle."

"Fingerprints?" Raymond tried to look shocked, but now his face was red. He narrowed his eyes. "You're not really a P.A., are you?" he said to Frank.

"No. I'm a private investigator working for Mr. Tannenberg," Frank admitted. "But I'm not after Lisa," he added.

"Well, who *are* you after?" Raymond asked.

"I can't tell you. All I want you to do is make sure Lisa doesn't try anything today." Frank moved closer and lowered his voice. "If you do, then I won't tell Mort about the smoke machine."

Raymond nodded. "Okay, Frank. I'll do what I can."

Leaving Raymond, Frank went back to Joe, who'd taken a seat in the auditorium. He made sure to be a few rows away from most of the extras.

"Is Raymond going to help?" Joe asked.

"Keep your fingers crossed."

Joe held up his crossed fingers. "What now?"

"Stay right where you are, and don't take your eyes off Sid," Frank instructed.

"Got it," Joe replied, and settled back to keep watch.

The first few hours were sheer chaos. Even with Sid helping Peter, it took numerous rehearsals before director March decided to go for a first take. Finally, Peter's voice boomed through the megaphone, "Quiet on the set!"

Frank saw that the camera was set up on the left side of the stage. It would start with a shot of the audience and then pan up to a box seat stage right. In that box stood Lisa and a stunt artist playing the deranged chemical engineer. The stunt artist was supposed to knock Lisa down, grab a nearby rope, and swing across the stage. At a precise moment, Lisa would pull out a rifle and shoot the rope. The engineer would fall to the stage, wounded.

"Mort wants to do it all in a long shot first," Charlie complained to Frank as he came up beside him. "I just hope we don't spend the whole day trying to get one shot."

Just as the camera was about to roll, a piece of scenery on stage collapsed. It took only a few minutes to repair, but it was long enough to make Mort furious. Finally, March yelled, "Action," and the camera rolled.

Joe held his breath. The stunt artist swung, and Lisa's gun went off. The stunt artist fell to the stage. March yelled "Cut and print!" Everyone applauded. It was a perfect take.

The crew shot two more successful takes and then spent the rest of the morning preparing for close-ups.

About midafternoon, Joe noticed Sid Renfield leaving the theater. He signaled to Frank to come over.

"He just left, Frank," Joe said as his brother took a seat next to him in the audience.

"I kind of thought he would," Frank said. "How are you feeling?"

146

"A lot better."

"Good. Here's the plan." Frank leaned close to Joe and lowered his voice. "When Sid comes back, I want you to check out Mort's Mercedes. I'm pretty sure you'll find that Sid tampered with the brakes."

"Right," Joe said. "Just like in the movie."

Frank nodded grimly. "Except you'll be fixing it. But Sid won't know that. After you check Mort's car," he went on, "take care of *Sid's* car with this." He handed Joe a paper sack filled with sand he'd taken from one of the sandbags. "Put all of it in his gas tank."

Joe sneaked out of the theater and Frank went back to work. About fifteen minutes later, Joe came backstage.

"Done?" Frank asked.

"Done," Joe answered. "And guess what? Sid drives a Jeep. And you'll never guess who I ran into in the parking lot."

"Who?"

"Cindy Langly."

"Great," Frank said, straightening a cable. "If Mort sees her, he'll go ballistic."

"I don't think we'll have to worry about that," Joe told him.

"Why? What did you do?"

"I tipped off a security guard. The one who is seven feet tall," Joe said with a laugh. "I think she's talking to him right now."

Frank smiled. "Nice work, Joe. And interesting

about Sid owning a Jeep. He must have been following us the other night."

There were some delays in the afternoon, but none of them were serious. Lisa remained on her best behavior, Cindy stayed away, and Mort was pleased with the day's work.

At 7:30 P.M., director March yelled, "It's a wrap." The crew went into high gear packing up the lights and scenery. Some of the actors hung around, chatting with Mort. Others just left. Frank kept a close eye on Sid. For a while the executive producer helped supervise the crew, then he said good-bye to Mort and walked out of the theater.

Frank rushed over to Mort and pulled him aside. It was time to go into his act. There was no point in telling Mort their suspicions yet. The producer would undoubtedly confront Sid, and Sid would just deny everything. Frank knew they didn't have any concrete proof. He hoped this plan would force Sid into a confession.

"I think we'd better go now," Frank said urgently.

"What's the rush?" Mort asked.

"We just got a phone call. Someone threatened your life."

"What?" Mort said, shocked.

"Come on," Frank insisted. "Joe and I will drive you home."

Joe followed Frank and Mort out of the theater and into the parking lot. Mort unlocked the doors to his Mercedes.

"Let me drive," Frank urged. "If we're followed, I'll know what to do." Mort agreed and got into the backseat beside Joe.

Just before they reached the bridge, they spotted Sid's Jeep on the side of the road. *The plan is working so far,* Frank thought as he pulled up beside it. He and Mort got out and walked over to Sid, who was peering under the Jeep's hood.

"Car trouble?" Frank asked innocently.

"Yeah," Sid said, straightening up. "It just died on me."

"Forget about it," Mort said. "We'll drive you home, and I'll send somebody out here tomorrow to take care of it for you."

Sid's face turned pale. "No, I don't think so," he said. "I'll call for a tow truck and . . ."

"You could be stuck waiting for hours," Frank said.

"Besides," Joe added, looking meaningfully at Mort. "You never know who could come along while you're stranded here in the dark."

"The kid's right," Mort said. He grabbed Sid's arm and escorted him to the Mercedes.

"Really, Mort," Sid insisted, "I'd rather stay with my car."

"Don't be ridiculous," Mort said. "You're coming with us."

Joe thought Sid looked like a trapped rat. There was no way he could keep refusing Mort's offer without arousing suspicion.

Mort dragged Sid over to the Mercedes. Joe

went around to the passenger side and got into the front seat. Mort slid into the back and looked expectantly at Sid. Sid didn't move, sweat breaking out across his forehead.

Mort stuck his head out the door. "What are you waiting for?" he barked. "Get in!"

Frank leaned against the hood of the car and watched Sid. The executive producer looked nervously at Mort and then at Frank.

"What's wrong with you?" Mort demanded. "Get in so we can get out of here!"

"Sid," Frank said evenly, "why don't you tell Mort why you don't want to get into the car."

"I . . . I . . ." Sid stammered.

Joe got back out of the car. "Don't you like to drive in cars without brakes?" Joe asked. He grabbed a small bag off the dashboard and put it down on top of the Mercedes. "And what about this?" Sid's face crumpled.

"Will someone tell me what's going on?" Mort shouted, climbing out of the car.

Joe opened the bag and held up a small device. "What's that?" Mort demanded.

"It's a small detonator with a timer on it," Frank said. "Mr. Renfield planted it under your car along with some explosives. He also drained the brake fluid."

"What?" Mort said, completely astonished.

"You tricked me!" Sid said, shaking his head.

Mort stared at Sid, his eyes wide. "You wanted to kill me, Sid?" he asked slowly.

Sid took a handkerchief out of his pocket and mopped his face. He didn't say anything.

"I'm afraid he did," Frank said to Mort. "If Mr. Renfield's plan had worked, the brakes would have failed, you'd be tumbling over the edge of the cliff, and your car would be exploding just about now."

"The last scene of *End of the Road!*" Mort croaked out. He was clearly astonished. "Why, Sid? What did I ever do to you?"

"Don't try to play the betrayed friend, Mort," Sid said angrily. "It's way out of character. You're as ruthless as they come. After thirty years, you dumped me for a kid fresh out of film school." Sid's voice grew louder. "You didn't think I could handle the set anymore! But I showed you, didn't I?" he said, laughing bitterly. "I showed you!"

"I can't believe it," Mort said later as he and the Hardys entered his den. They'd made one stop along the way—at a police station, where they'd left Sid Renfield.

"I just can't believe it," Mort said again, shaking his head. "Sid Renfield wanted to kill me."

Mort plopped down on the couch next to Chet, who was still house-sitting. "I've got to hand it to you boys," he said. "You saved my life."

"It was Sid Renfield?" Chet asked, excited.

"Yep," Joe said.

Chet grabbed a few Cheez Doodles from a bowl on the coffee table and stuffed them into his mouth. "How'd you figure it out?" he asked.

151

"Good question," Mort said.

"Well, we knew we were looking for someone with the expertise to pull off the stunts. And someone who had access to everything, including Mr. Tannenberg's old films," Frank explained.

"That's how he got the voice on the answering machine," Joe continued. "He edited pieces of the soundtracks from your wife's movies."

"But why'd he do it?" Chet asked.

"The motive. That was the hard part," Frank said. "But thanks to you, Chet, I found the answer in one of Cindy Langly's articles."

Mort's expression turned grim. "Don't mention that name in this house."

"Sorry," Frank said. "Anyway, Sid felt betrayed when Mort took away his authority and had him handle only the old movies. And he decided to get his revenge."

"I never imagined it meant that much to him," Mort said thoughtfully.

"Well, it did," Frank said. "You know, it might be a good idea to pay more attention to the way you treat people."

"You could be right," Mort said, almost in a whisper.

"Yeah," Joe joined in, "you could let Lisa out of her contract."

Mort looked almost embarrassed. "Maybe I haven't treated the kid fairly," he admitted. "I'll have to think about it."

"Well, that's your business," Frank added. "It's getting late and we have to go. Our parents are getting back tonight, and we have a room to straighten up. Come on, Chet."

"But, Frank, can't we stay a little longer?" Chet pleaded. "I've got this great idea for a movie and I want to tell Mr. T. all about it."

Frank and Joe exchanged glances. Mort laughed. "Everyone wants to be in show biz!" he said.

"It's all about three detectives who—" Chet began eagerly.

"No more movies!" Joe cut him off. He and Frank each grabbed one of Chet's arms and hoisted him off the couch, spilling Cheez Doodles everywhere.

"Hmmm," Mort said thoughtfully. "I've got some old mysteries I could rerelease. Not a bad idea." He looked at the three boys and chuckled. "But no more surprise endings for me!"

"At least not until next time!" Frank said.

NANCY DREW® MYSTERY STORIES By Carolyn Keene